Family Weave

Lee Sowder

Family Weave

Lee Sowder

Torchflame Books

Durham, NC

Published 2021, by Torchflame Books
an Imprint of Light Messages
www.lightmessages.com
Durham, NC 27713 USA
SAN: 920-9298

Paperback ISBN: 978-1-61153-407-8
E-book ISBN: 978-1-61153-408-5
Library of Congress Control Number: 2020923579

For my mother,
Eloise Davis Sowder

1

Ready

WHEN MAMA CALLS AND SAYS SHE LOST HER CANE again, I am getting ready to leave for book club, the neighborhood gathering where the same women talk about the book and the same women drink too much and the same women bring the chips and salsa or orange salad with raisins every month. I fell into the paper products or bottle of chardonnay group of women who nod along and don't say a word. The book this month was 'Small, Great Things' by Jodi Picoult, and even though I had not read it, I had read enough of Jodi Picoult to feel confident enough to nod while the others made their comments. I'm not what you would call a small talker, but I do recognize my need to show my face out and about every once in a while, and that does keep my sister Perk from nagging me to get out more. Besides, every woman in her sixties knows enough of living to know sometimes even bad company is better than no company at all, if for nothing more than reminding herself what good company she can be all on her own.

By the time I hang up with Mama, I've already put the bottle of Sutter Chardonnay back in the refrigerator and am headed for the front door, my mind rolling over the worries of Mama not having her cane, of her falling or cracking her head on the floor of the apartment. I can see each one of them plain as day. I hurry out of the house with a pit sitting heavy in my stomach, not quite a panic, but growing that way. Mama is not but a few miles down the road, but at 96 years old you just never know.

The best thing my sister and I ever did was to move Mama out of her house in Roanoke after she fell a few years back, pack up her things and move her here, to Richmond and into Serenity, a senior solutions complex up the street from me. There is a fine line between abruptly taking control of a parent's life and trying to disguise the fact that you are taking control of a parent's life for as long as is possible. It's what my sister Perk likes to call Management by Crisis. It is why we waited so long, all the while knowing Mama was but a fall away from needing us to step in, take charge. That time came after Mama was admitted to Carilion Memorial Hospital, drugged up and laid out in a private room with a fractured collarbone and bruises up and down her body, all from tripping over her own feet. Mama always says you make your own luck, but it was just dumb luck her housekeeper Lilly came that morning and found Mama lying beside her bed, conscious enough to smile and say, "I must look a sight."

Lilly called 911 and then called Perk in Richmond, and within a span of five minutes Perk called me and told her husband Teddy to go fill up the car because we were all driving to Roanoke. On the outside it might have looked like Perk and I were watching our Mama's life from afar, but the truth of it was that we always had a plan, we just needed a crisis to rise up before we could put that plan into action. And that plan was moving Mama to Richmond to be near us. Family takes care of family.

In the five days Mama was in the hospital, Perk and Teddy and I got the old house closed up and the mail forwarded and the paper stopped, and all the while I worried and panicked and practically chewed off the inside of my cheek thinking about Mama in pain and helpless in the hospital. Perk, on the other hand, wasn't worried one bit. She never is. "What good does worrying do?" she'll tell me. "You can't fix a thing with a worry." I do believe Perk would remove that word from the dictionary, she finds it so useless. I got all the worrying genes in our family.

You can tell just looking at us that Perk and I are as different as night and day. My sister is almost six feet tall with natural red hair that has started fading but doesn't have but a strand or two of white, even at sixty-eight years old. I'm the short one, barely five-three and gray headed from the time I turned sixty. Perk says if I didn't worry so much my hair would have stayed brown, but I just think its common sense to view the world in terms of the danger it holds. Between Perk and Teddy, you would think there had never been a war or a disease or any terrible thing to happen in this world. In the forty-odd years Perk has been married to Teddy, I don't believe I've heard them worry over a single thing but money, earning enough money to raise their son James or buy a house. Anything else just doesn't seem worthwhile to them. "Why worry if you can't do a thing about it?" Perk likes to say about any little thing I am fretting over. Even though I never had children or got married, I have come to think I carry enough worry for the three of us. Worrying comes as natural to me now as it did when I was a child.

The day before we moved Mama out of Roanoke, Perk and I were sitting at the kitchen table in Mama's house, our childhood home, while Teddy picked up the sandwiches from the deli down the street. Roanoke has grown from a small railroad town when we were growing up to a full-fledged city now, a hub for southwestern Virginians to move to for the railroad, for the medical school, and for the mountain roots they left and then ran back to once they were grown. Perk and I never did (come back, that is), but then Mama was always here, on Yellow Mountain, and it seemed like we were always coming home to see her.

"I'm not sure we should be moving Mama to Richmond, Perk. I mean, I could come back here and take care of her," I said to Perk as we sat at Mama's kitchen table.

"Pauline, you know as well as I do Mama can't live alone anymore. Do you want to move back to Roanoke?"

I thought about that for a second. I did love Roanoke, but I had my own home in Richmond. I'd put down my roots there, alongside Perk and Teddy. "No, but I could stay until Mama healed up and…"

"Pauline, if we bring Mama back to this house we are never going to get her to leave. We both know she is going to fall again or get lost driving that car of hers, and she shouldn't be driving. No ninety-six-year old should be driving. If we have any hope of moving Mama to Richmond for good, we need to strike while the iron is hot."

"I know. I just hate what's coming, Perk." I feel a tightening in my stomach, a worry running up and around my neck. I can see Mama in that hospital bed, alone, and my mind begins to race with worry, what she needs, how she feels.

"We should be at the hospital, looking out for Mama." I said as I worried my hands on the table, rubbing the smoothed pine I'd refinished almost sixty years ago.

"Pauline, we just spent four hours there and all she did was sleep. She is as safe as she can be in that hospital. We'll be lucky if they keep her a while longer so we can be ready to move her."

"Those nurses get busy, Perk. What if she wakes up scared and tries to get out of bed and falls again? Don't you think we should be there? You know as well as I do, family sees you through all the times, good and bad." Perk looked at me then like I had said the most inconsequential thing, a look that said, "this is not worthy of discussion." I felt my face heating up. Sitting there, we could have been ten and thirteen, facing off and fighting over who was going to do the dishes. The only difference now was the shared years in between then and now. The older I get the more I stop looking for the differences we have and appreciate instead the love we've shared all these years later.

As cold-hearted as Perk sounded to me then, hers were the only words now that calmed me down. When we were kids, she could talk a circle around my worry in her matter of fact way, like explaining that the communists couldn't burn our house down because they lived in another country. Perk's logic made me mad back then, and we would fight over who was right, me with my fists clenching, shouting that she was wrong, that airplanes could fly the communists right over Yellow Mountain, and Perk with those folded arms, rolling her eyes, calling me stupid and walking away, both of us convinced we were right. Back then I cared so much about convincing Perk and she didn't care one bit about convincing me back. Now Perk's logic acts like a balm, something I can depend on when my worry is pounding against my chest, overwhelming me with a helplessness that seems like it is going to be too much for me to take.

When Mama was discharged, we drove her back to Richmond. She had been too drugged up from the pain to notice much of where we were driving, and when we finally pulled up in front of my house, all she said was, "Well that took long enough."

I suppose in the back of both our minds Perk and I had known what would come first. I had the one-story home,

Perk and Teddy's house a four square with the bedrooms at the top of a long set of steps. Mama moved into my guest bedroom, and for the next five weeks my life was caring for Mama. I had thought overseeing Mama's care would suit me, but I was wrong. Having Mama in my house, fretting over her every move and every pain and every meal, plucked out my last nerve. I woke up in the mornings panicked that Mama had fallen out of bed at night, and I then proceeded to find one thing or another to worry my nerves concerning her well-being until I closed my eyes at night.

The lightbulbs in my house were always too dim. That's when the complaints started. I'd forgotten how critical Mama could be about anything outside of her own way of doing things, like using 200-watt bulbs in every room in her house, lighting up that three-story brick house in Roanoke like a Christmas tree every night.

"Why do you keep it so dark in here?" Mama would say, even after I switched out my 60-watt bulbs to 100-watt and bought her a standup lamp at Target. The meals I served were never hot enough, even with the steam circling the plate. One evening, I was helping Mama down to the chair for dinner and I jostled her bad shoulder. She let out such a groan my heart twisted in a panic.

"Mama, I am so sorry. Can I get you a Tylenol?"

"No, Pauline," Mama snapped, "you take more pills than is good for you."

I could feel my face heating red hot and my neck muscles stiffen. The helplessness I felt rushed over me like a tidal wave. I breathed in several calming breaths and didn't say a word. Mama sat stiffly in her chair, her jaw set to argue anything else I had to say.

"Can I get an extra pillow?" I finally asked as sweetly as I could through my clenched teeth.

"Good Lord, Pauline. Just pour me a glass of wine." Mama shot a look that could have sliced a ham thin as paper.

"Mama, the doctors don't want you drinking alcohol while you are taking medicine for the pain."

"Fine with me. I don't like that medicine anyway. Do I have to come pour my glass myself?" Mama was as clear-eyed angry as I had seen her since the day I explained she wasn't going back to Roanoke. That day I saw Mama struggle to hold conflicting concepts, the joy of finally living near her daughters, the pain of leaving her lifelong home, and the anger that I was telling her what to do. That day her anger came through. Today, I decided right then I wasn't going to argue.

"Mama, we're having your favorite, lasagna. And yes, I am bringing your wine. Just hold your horses." I sighed and rubbed her good shoulder softly, and even though she flinched, Mama's face softened, and I could see just a shade of smile curling her lips.

Mama never thought a thing was wrong with her, and it took the nurse questioning her about her bladder movements before we realized she had a urinary tract infection. After I picked up the prescription at the Kroger pharmacy and saw the size of the pills, I worried myself into a panic that she wouldn't be able to swallow them. I ended up cutting each pill into four pieces and making Mama stand at the kitchen sink with a tall glass of water until she swallowed all of them. For ten days we had a daily battle.

"Mama, you have got to take your pills if you don't want to end up in the hospital."

"I am fine, Pauline. I do not need to take pills."

"Fine, Mama. But we don't drink a glass of wine tonight if you haven't taken your pills."

"Quit being so bossy, Pauline." Mama would set her jaw and shoot me a look and I would shoot her a look right back, the both of us in a showdown, neither of us even blinking. Finally, Mama would heave a sigh and look off at nothing for a second, then look back at me with a twinkle in her eyes like I had just told her the funniest joke in the world, shake her head, and steady herself with her cane before walking into the kitchen to take the pills. We could have been a couple of parrots talking back and forth, every day, saying the same words, over and over.

I would have thought the days after she finished her prescription would be easier, but it turned out I was wrong. As Mama's body got stronger, her will power did too. When Mama first moved in and I would ask her how she was feeling, Mama would say, "Pauline, I've got a sore arm, I'm not dying."

"No," I'd say, "but you aren't going to get better if you don't take care of yourself."

Mama would give me a little smile, twinkling those blue eyes still blurry from the Tylenol 3, and mutter softly, "Leave me alone," without a bit of fight left in her, all the while holding out her arm so I could help her back into her bed.

As the days turned to weeks and Mama's shoulder healed, she stopped groaning with pain. Instead, Mama asked me ten times a day when I was taking her back to Roanoke. It became a refrain as common as me asking her ten times a day how she was feeling. Perk and I had already found a realtor to sell Mama's house, but we waited to list until we had a better idea where Mama was going to live. One of the smartest things Perk did was to get power of attorney documents signed once we found out Mama had been falling, back when she was in her eighties. Even then we were preparing ourselves as best we could, considering how independent our Mama was.

There is just so much change an elderly woman should have to deal with at any one time.

My daily calls to Perk included what Mama had eaten, how she slept, and what the occupational and physical therapists coming to the house had done on any particular day. Between Mama staying with me and the therapists and visiting nurse stopping by, I had more company in those five weeks than I had had in five years, and that, in the end, wore me down the most. I tried to get Perk and Teddy over for dinner with Mama and me, but every time I asked Perk said she was busy, busy with a prayer circle or a volunteer meeting at the church. I didn't say it to Perk, but I was thinking it: *Perk's too busy for her own Mama, too busy to help me out.* That thought kept building inside me to where I was gritting my teeth every time we talked.

I already mentioned I am not a small talker, and the comings and goings of Mama's medical team kept me on edge as much as worrying how Mama was mending. There was Clarice, the occupational therapist with the giant feet who always smelled like patchouli incense and told me every time she arrived I looked just like her cousin Terry in North Carolina. Clarice broke my kitchen sink hose the first week trying to get Mama to stretch her arm to wash a glass out. Then there was Penny, the nurse who always arrived late and never apologized, just stepped through the door and started barking orders at Mama. She was a tiny woman with a long gray ponytail who never seemed to smile, and Mama and I both agreed she wasn't cut out to be a nurse. Between the constant comings and goings of those women and Mama's groans and gripes at any little thing, muscles I never knew existed were tightening up in my neck to where I couldn't even turn to the side without feeling stiff. Daily headaches and a sour stomach became as commonplace as those women knocking on my door.

After Mama settled in and was able to move around my house on her own, I drove over to Perk's to have a come to Jesus discussion about Mama. We talked on the phone every day, but Perk hadn't stopped by to see Mama since we drove back from Roanoke, and that had been a few weeks ago. Perk was still dressed in her Sunday suit and earrings, and was kicking off her high heels when I walked in.

"What's the occasion?" I could feel my face heating just seeing Perk all dressed up, going about her life like nothing at all. My temper was not cool and collected. I was mad.

"I told you last night, that church meeting with the new minister, Pauline. Reverend Thompson is just wonderful. He was a missionary in Africa and has all sorts of ideas for community outreach. I told Teddy we need to volunteer."

"Perk, what about Mama? You can't even find time to come over and help out." I felt my breath catch in my throat. Clenching my fists, I looked over at Perk and said, "I'm about to crack open. I don't think you have one clue, but I can tell you what, the day is coming that I'm going to drive Mama right over with that suitcase of hers and leave her sitting in your living room. See how you like caring for her."

Perk was watching me, not saying a word. We faced off until finally she walked over and put her arms around me and squeezed.

"I'm sorry, Pauline. I didn't know it was that bad. I wanted to give you and Mama time to get used to living together. Teddy said you two wouldn't last a week, but I told him you wanted to take care of Mama."

"I did. I just didn't know how hard it would be on me. My nerves are so worn down I am afraid I'll say something really ugly to Mama or worse, just walk out my own door and never come back. Besides, you could've come over Perk, helped me out instead of sitting back going to church meetings and waiting for me to complain. You're her daughter too." Words were running fast out of my mouth as if they had been piling up waiting for the door to open. My breathing was harder, shorter, with gasps and gulps as I waited for Perk to talk. The last thing on my mind had been blaming Perk for my nerves unraveling, until right now, when the words came like a spitting fire. "I have a life too, Perk."

"Of course you do. I wouldn't be a good sister if I didn't know that and want you living it."

My breathing slowed. Perk and I sat at her kitchen table, both our faces softer now, watching the other.

"I know this is hard on you, Pauline," Perk finally said, "and I'll take care of this. But you have got to speak up. We talk every night, and all I have heard is everything is fine. I am no mind reader, and it is not up to me to figure out what you are thinking. Just talk to me. You've told me, now I'll take care of it."

I knew Perk was right. I have never been one to express a whole lot of feeling until that feeling builds inside of me and has no room left but to come tumbling out. I remember that day when I was eight years old and Perk was eleven, after Daddy died, when Perk cried and cried and I held back my tears, clenching my fists, swallowing hard to keep down the heavy pit spreading grief like a fearful thing deep inside me. All the while she was letting out her grief, I was holding it all in, thinking if I didn't show it, all that pain would go away.

That summer when Daddy died, the days and months before, Mama, Perk, and I would visit the downtown hospital and the room where he laid, growing thinner and paler, so much so the ghost of him would greet us at the door. I came to dread those visits and the fears that would rise in me, fears that I couldn't change what was happening inside that room, that death was in that room and on my Daddy's pasty face. While Mama and Perk sat beside Daddy and held his hand, I would sit in his wheelchair and roll myself up and down the hallway, while the nurses smiled and never told me to stop.

In the last remaining summer months after Daddy died, Mama and Perk and I would walk as if in a coma across the alley to Granny and Grandaddy's house. On a Saturday night, we would sit in their backyard under the crabapple tree, eating corn on the cob and fried chicken and yeast rolls with our cousins, each of us given a turn churning the homemade ice cream while the dry ice smoked around the wooden bucket and the metal churn grew thick with frozen cream and peaches. Walking home, lightening bugs shining up and down the alley, Perk and Mama would walk hand in hand as I plotted on ahead, the night falling all around us.

Perk kept on crying for years, at just about the drop of a hat, but I walled off every one of my tears and only let them loose when I was alone. We had an old pine kitchen table a friend of Daddy's made for Mama and Daddy when they got married. It had a rough, rounded top and legs crisscrossed like a picnic table, and matching pine benches. For meals, Daddy and I sat on one bench, and Mama and Perk on the other. In the weeks after Daddy died, I took to sanding that table, rubbing the top over and over in the evenings, while Mama and Perk watched television upstairs. I cried at that table every night, rubbing down the pine. I told Mama I was going to refinish it and she acted like that was the most special thing in the world I could do. Even then, making Mama proud lifted my heart.

Nights after the dishes were washed and the kitchen cleaned, I sat on the bench and sanded, full of purpose. I cried at the table, for my Daddy and missing my Daddy, afraid of feeling the hurt in my eight-year-old heart. Those nights, Mama or Perk or the both of them would come down and watch me work, Mama sometimes asking if I wanted to talk about Daddy. I never did. The both of them would see my red eyes and not say a thing about that. It took me two years to finish that table. I switched sandpaper from rough to fine and then extra-fine steel wool and finally a brush to apply the light satin stain Mama and I picked out at the hardware store. I still remember the look of joy lighting Mama's eyes when it was finally complete.

I couldn't tell you much about the years after Daddy died. I lived my days in a fog, split in two, going to school and playing with friends, pasting in scrapbooks and staying up late at slumber parties. Then, at home with Perk and Mama, I cried at my kitchen table, the grief inside me growing. I walked the rest of those childhood years apart from everybody outside my family, Daddy's death the wall that kept me on the other side from friends. I would joke and act silly with them, never saying one word about the hole in my heart. When my best friend Margaret asked me what it was like not having a daddy, I just rolled my eyes, acting bored, and told her I didn't think about him, didn't want to talk about him. Even then, I was learning to keep my feelings private, even from myself. There is something fierce that grows inside a child living outside a ring of friends, at best an independence and at worst an anger. Those childhood years I was growing both.

Perk spent those years after Daddy died learning to express her feelings and learning to love herself for doing just that. She would cry and talk about Daddy to Mama, and the more she did it the more I resented her for getting all of Mama's attention. I picked fights with her for no reason at all other than to stop her from talking about Daddy. She would start talking about Daddy at the dinner table and my stomach would turn, tighten. All I would see was that pasty face in the hospital room, and the fear would start rising inside me. Mama would look across the table and smile, nod at me and just say, "We're going to be all right, sweetie," then get up and clear the table.

Sitting at Perk's kitchen table, I heard Perk's words, though, "I'll take care of it," and my shoulders dropped a little with relief. And as hard as it has ever been for me to ask for help, my shoulders dropped a little more once I told her I needed it.

"Well, I wish I knew five weeks ago that caring for the elderly was not a job skill I can claim. And Mama is a test for even the highly qualified," I said.

We both laughed, and I stood up and hugged Perk. "Love you," I said and turned around to head home to Mama.

"Pauline, call me when you need help. I love you." Perk stood by her front door and waved until my car was pointed down the street to home.

That next day Perk called back and told me what all she had found out about Serenity, the senior solutions community up the street from me. We could rent Mama a two-bedroom apartment in their independent living building and hire aides to come in for health checks as often as we needed them. The apartment was big enough to hold her most cherished antiques and paintings, and the second bedroom would give Perk and I a room to stay in if we needed to. We signed the lease on the same day, and Perk and Teddy drove a U-Haul to Roanoke and packed up as much of Mama's special things as would fit in a two-bedroom apartment. For once I was relieved to stay back with Mama, leaving Perk and Teddy to begin the clearing out of our childhood home, the three-story brick house up against the base of Yellow Mountain. Just the thought of seeing the house empty sent a fear shooting through me.

Mama and Daddy had bought the lot from Granny and Grandaddy when they married. They built our house on a red clay hill that backed up to Yellow Mountain. The basement had a pair of bay windows that looked out on the sloping backyard, the alley lined with Granny's orange tiger lilies, and a row of chestnut trees in Granny and Grandaddy's side yard. Beyond, Yellow Mountain rose up. My bedroom faced the mountain and the back of Granny and Grandaddy's red Tudor brick house. I could see out my window when Grandaddy was pulling into the driveway from the hospital where he worked as a surgeon, or when Granny was backing her Cadillac out to go shopping downtown. I could open my window and call out through the screen, "Hey Granny," and not even raise my voice. Sound carried along the mountainside like you were sitting in the same room.

All through my childhood, Granny and Grandaddy's house was like an extension of our house, and we all went back and forth at any time of the day. Our living room had wide pine floors and the mountain was framed like a picture along the wide bay window. Mama and Daddy were big on windows when they built our house, and every room facing the mountain had wide, tall windows. I could be washing dishes in the kitchen and see Yellow Mountain, Granny and Grandaddy's house, and the road winding up the mountain. Over the years, Mama bought antiques to fill our house from the old people Granny knew, and the relatives too old to keep their houses, and sometimes, from the antique store downtown. The only pieces of furniture that weren't antiques in our house were the long green, satin covered couch that sat in the living room, long enough to seat six people and with cushions that sprang down when you sat, and the kitchen table. Every one of those antiques told a story, and all you had to do was ask Mama about this one or that one and she would tell you. Over the years those antiques told our stories too, held all of our memories.

Not a minute of it all seemed real to me until we had unpacked the U-Haul – not the rushing to Roanoke, not the seeing Mama in the hospital, not even the days and weeks caring for her in my own house. Seeing Mama's furniture, though, unpacking only enough of her life as would fit in a two-bedroom apartment of blank white walls and cream-colored carpet, empty of memories, shook me hard. A sadness from deep inside awoke and took hold, a sadness that went back to when Daddy had died.

Perk watched me as together we moved the large Majorca painting into the apartment and said, "We'll do the best we can, Pauline. We'll make this her home." My eyes continued to water but I knew Perk was right, we'd do the best we could for Mama.

One thing I didn't take into account was Mama's ability to see the sunny side of any day. Not any time went by before Mama was calling that apartment home, sleeping in the same four poster bed she and Daddy had slept in before he died, and the fifty odd years since by herself. Using the same metal coffee pot to heat up leftover Mr. Coffee, snacking on the same Little Debbie honey buns and fresh cantaloupe for breakfast, Mama thrived on the comforts of her routines.

Once I hang up with Mama, I call Sheri who is hosting book club tonight So many of these women prefer texting but I do not. I find it rude, and also my phone has tiny letters that are difficult to see.

"Sheri, I hate to miss tonight, but Mama lost her cane and I need to go find it."

"Oh Pauline, you are such a good daughter. You know CVS sells them?"

"I know, but Mama is particular."

"Well, we will miss seeing your cheerful face, but I understand. See you next month?"

"Oh yes. And could you let me know the book for next month?"

"I will. I am going to suggest another Jodi Picoult since everyone likes her so much."

"Yes, everyone loves Jodi. Bye now, Sheri, and thanks." I hang up before Sheri asks me how I liked the book.

By the time I get to Mama's apartment, she's sitting on her bed, the television on the dresser blasting out Wheel of Fortune so you can hear all the way out in the hallway.

"Hey, Mama, did you find your cane?" I say as I peek my head into her bedroom.

Mama looks over at me, smiling. "Pauline, what are you doing here?"

I speak before I have a chance to catch myself, "You called me. Your cane, you lost your cane?"

Mama's eyes hold just a touch of empty before they sharpen back. "Oh that, well I don't need a cane."

I take my deep breath, the one Perk told me to take anytime Mama loses touch. The one I take so I don't end up arguing. "Mama, I'll be right back."

I start retracing her steps, the well-worn route Mama takes every day down the halls and breezeways, the flights of stairs she climbs, and the heavy fire doors she pushes open using her whole body weight, all hundred-and-two pounds of stooped shoulders and brittle bird bones, using muscle memory from back when her daddy told her that climbing stairs would keep her healthy.

This time she's left her cane in the elevator. I would have found it a lot sooner if I hadn't taken the first elevator and the cane took the other one. It's real easy to spot, with four little rubber prongs at the bottom that look like little toes sticking out, and a brown and gold paisley design running up the cane, the one she bought from CVS after falling in her backyard in Roanoke five years ago. Classy, like everything else about Mama, inside and out. Growing up, I never knew her to leave the house without first applying her lipstick and blush, attaching her clip-on earrings, and draping one of her many matching silk scarfs loosely around her neck. Over the years Mama's range of motion has shrunk to where she can't pull a dress over her head, put a knit blouse on, or open and close tiny buttons. But Mama still dresses better than most folks do, and applies lipstick anytime she goes on a walk. These days most of her slacks are baggy, even though I keep taking them to the cleaners to take in, but she will always wear a tasteful blouse and blazer. When I bring the cane back to her apartment and tell her where I've found it, she laughs.

"Oh, those elevators are so crowded. I must've left it trying to get out the door." Mama smiles. She is a woman of routine, but sometimes she does like to mix it up, and when she does, the change as natural to her as the routine. It's the rest of us that can't keep up.

I still remember the time Dorothy, the mid-day aide, found Mama in the stairwell between the sixth and seventh floors, leaned up against the fire door. When I asked Mama why she took the fire stairs, she said she got tired of waiting for the elevator.

"Pauline, stairs are meant to be used. Your grandaddy always said that to avoid becoming a constitutional inadequate you need to keep the blood pumping, keep moving, avoid elevators, and use the stairs. Every one of my friends died constitutional inadequates because they stopped moving."

"Mama, your senior solutions team doesn't like you using those stairs, they think it's dangerous, and no one would know if you fell." Just the thought of Mama stranded in the fire exit, alone and unable to move, sent me into panic, that mix of pressure in my stomach and teeth grinding that comes whenever I feel I have lost control of helping Mama. I had looked at her hard then and said, "You could fall and break your skull and I couldn't help you."

"Don't be silly, I have no intention of falling." Mama shook her head and smiled, satisfied that would end the discussion.

Both Perk and Mama had a way of dismissing my worries, glossing over the terrible outcomes I imagined and dwelling on what was always right in front of them. That was as natural for them as worrying over every possible tragedy was for me.

"Well," I sighed, knowing this was a debate I wasn't going to win, "I think it's okay then."

"Pauline, of course it's all right, that's what I do." Mama shook her head then and laughed, looking at me like I had just said the most inconsequential thing in the entire world. For a moment, I wasn't 65 anymore, but a girl of 10 or 12. A few years after Daddy died, I decided Mama needed to re-marry. We needed another Daddy to take care of us, and I told her so one night when she was tucking me in.

"Mama, I found a husband for you. Up the street, Mr. Miller is rich and has two dogs. And we need someone to take care of us."

Mama had looked at me and before I could breathe again, she started laughing, and kept laughing so long I sat up, angry, and said, "What are you laughing at?"

"Oh Pauline, we don't need anyone to take care of us. And honey, you don't marry a man to have him take care of you.

You marry him because you love him. And, honey, I loved your Daddy and he is the only man I will ever love." She looked at me then and smiled. "But thank you, honey. You are a big help to me."

Today, I manage not to scold Mama and leave her happily watching Jeopardy with her cane sitting right beside the bed. I leave her apartment still doing my calming breaths. Several years ago, Blue Cross, where I worked in the claims processing department from right out of college to the day I retired, offered a free class at lunchtime that taught you to relax. Breathing was big in that class, and when I told Perk about it, she said, "Well, I think that sounds a lot like the breathing I did when I was having James. It helped me through the birthing pain. You might as well try it." I took the class a few times and then they started another one where you did exercises, and I decided to take walks instead.

I've already crossed off going to book club late, and I point my car home. I am a woman who believes in the comforts of home, and as I walk through my front door my mind goes straight to the chilled glass of Suters I am going to pour myself, right after I feed the cats. Family takes care of family, and the cats are included. A chicken pesto Lean Cuisine and a glass of wine later, I slip into my nightgown and turn up the heated mattress pad on my bed. Law and Order reruns are playing on the USA channel, and I settle back in bed and watch them until my eyes start to close. For now, at least, a crisis has been averted, and my sleep is peaceful.

2

Pauline

I WAKE UP LIKE I ALWAYS DO BEFORE SEVEN, but this morning there is a current in the air, a feeling that something is different. My two cats, Jimbo and Sassy, are sound asleep at the foot of the bed. I have a nice home, paid for, with enough room to move around in and never once see a corner out of place. It is a joy of living alone. Perk might call me up and say, "Come on Pauline, Teddy and I are fixing a pot roast and it's too much food for just the two of us." And I might ride over, but I might just stay right here instead. It takes twice as long to get to Mama's from Perk's house, and you just never know.

I live my life on call. The last time I got a call from Laura, the senior solutions supervisor, she told me Mama had caught the oven on fire. Mama had opened a bag of Cheetos cheese popcorn and a few pieces had spilled over onto the hot stovetop, smoking and setting off the fire alarm. Everything turned out fine, the maintenance man had been right there on her floor. But that Laura still called me, said she was concerned about Mama's safety, made it sound like Mama's life was in danger. She wanted to take off the knobs on Mama's stove. Perk and I did not agree. Mama is an independent sort. Widowed at 42 and raising two daughters on her own, she learned to do things her way. Instead, we just started bringing her groceries for the microwave. One thing you learn early in taking care of the elderly is to be flexible and creative. It makes all the difference.

Perk and I waited until Mama was settled in at Serenity before we sold her house in Roanoke. Mama's bank account was not a worry, but the extra money the sale brought in padded it fat. Neither of us wanted to do it, but the chore of looking after a house three hours away was more than either of us wanted to take on. Selling our house felt like an ending, a death. When I walked through that empty house one last time, there wasn't a memory left I could feel, except gazing at Yellow Mountain beyond the kitchen window.

Perk already had power of attorney, but she insisted Mama sign the contract, too. We picked a day when Mama woke clear-headed and bright. The three of us went to the apartment and sat with Mama in her living room. Her bay window looked out on a parking lot and Mama sat beside it. She listened as Perk explained why we had sold the house, that the depreciation of leaving a house empty and the wear and tear would lower the value. Mama had been a realtor for forty years, finally retiring when she turned eighty. She understood the facts, signed the contract, and asked us when we were going out to dinner. The three of us hugged her and left. Timing is everything when talking to the elderly.

Even as I lie here with this unsettling feeling, my bed is nice and cozy. I bought this heated mattress pad from Target the last time I went on a shopping spree. My store of choice has always been Target – with those wide aisles and that red everywhere, you can't help but feel alive when you walk through those doors. People can talk all they want about the Chinese taking over our economy and how we should all buy local. I prefer a bargain and I don't care where I get it. Deciding when to spend money is a true dilemma for us retirees, but you get used to it. Besides, processing Blue Cross major medical claims might not have been a fancy job, but my pension lets me shake a dollar or two now and again on just me. And I have plans. For one day. Makes no kind of sense taking a cruise now when Mama could need help. Anytime at all. I do have a cell phone, but you never know about coverage. Those dead zones are real. Perk would call me a worrier, but I prefer to think I'm just a realist. There is just so much you can do at any one time.

I lean over to turn off the mattress pad and for the tiniest moment feel a rush of warmth running down me, as if I have just taken a sip of something warm and delicious. Smiling, I get myself up and out of bed and walk down the hall. That's when I catch sight of what's next to the front door, or rather what's not next to it. I keep a pair of loafers right by the door in case I need to slip them on in a hurry to go take care of Mama. They aren't expensive, just old scratched up leather on the outside and a soft fleecy lining on the inside, hand-me-downs from Mama, the soles worn down and paper thin, now as much a part of me as they were a part of her. And this morning they are not there. Again.

It happened once before, a month ago. I had been out with my book club, discussing another Jodi Picoult novel. When I got home, my loafers were by the front door, like they always are. Perk called and told me about the trip she and Teddy were going to take down to Florida for a week. Perk kept asking why I didn't come along, and I had said no and then listened to her some more, and then I had said maybe, and finally I had said I'd sleep on it and talk to her in the morning. That night I had a dream. My mattress pad was set to eight and my body already thought it was down south, warm breezes blowing, coconut trees shading me from the sun. In my dream I was way out on this bright blue water, I think it was the ocean but calm, and I was in this sailboat and I didn't know how to drive it and I was looking at the shore. I could see Mama sitting on the beach, waving at me, smiling, wearing a straw hat with a wide brim. And Perk and Teddy were there too, over by the coconut trees, fussing about who was going to carry the coconuts back to the car. I remember thinking in my dream-state about how in the world was I going to get back there. And then the wind kicked up and this pretty yellow sail got real fat and there I went, away from them, away from shore. And I was driving the boat. That's when I woke up.

It happened that next morning, after I woke up uneasy, when I walked out to the hallway and stared at the space beside the front door. No loafers. I thought I must still be dreaming, and I didn't even make coffee, I just started hunting for those loafers. There are some belongings that take on meaning beyond being things; they hold cherished memories, more like living things inside you. Mama's loafers were that. That worn brown leather softened and faded over the years Mama wore them, and faded more in the few years since she gave them to me, bending and molding to my feet. All those years ago when Mama bought them at Saxon Shoes, she told Perk and me both, "You don't pinch pennies on shoes. Spend the money and buy high quality shoes. They have to carry you through this life."

I was six when Mama bought those loafers, and up until the day we moved her to Richmond you could find them in the kitchen, by the side door. Mama slipped them on to walk over to Granny and Grandaddy's house, or to take a walk with Daddy around the neighborhood with Perk and me. We'd walk up to Clermont Park, and Perk and I would swing while Daddy sat on a big rock to rest and Mama alternated swinging Perk then me. She never wore them anywhere fancy like to church or bridge club, but I could find her weeding the front hill or carrying out the trash in those loafers, then she would come in and carefully wipe them off with a rag. The day Daddy died, Mama got a call early in the morning from the hospital. She called Granny to come watch Perk and me and left the house wearing those loafers. It's the only time I can think of she wore them anywhere but around the neighborhood.

That morning the loafers disappeared from beside my front door, I looked in every corner of every room in my house, every closet, and even in the trash can, before I finally went back to my bedroom and felt a pull to look under my bed and saw them there, lined up in a perfect little row below the headboard. I lost touch for just a second, the floor I was kneeling on and the air I was breathing in both felt cool and warm at the same time. For a tiny second, I wasn't thinking at all, I was just feeling the cool and warm as I stared at those loafers. I sensed this warm light shining out from them, like staring into the kindest pair of eyes, full of love for me. It was the strangest thing and at the same time seemed as natural as the day. And the most surprising part of it all was that I wasn't afraid, not one bit.

When Perk and I were kids, after our Daddy died, our maid Hester used to say that she would hear him whistling through the front door like he used to do when he came home for lunch. Hester was part Cherokee and believed in spirits. She always told us she felt Daddy there in our house after he died. Perk scoffed at Hester when she told us Daddy was still in the house, watching out for us. She would tell Hester and me both dead people don't come back. Even back then, if Perk couldn't make sense of something, she decided it wasn't true. But I looked and listened for Daddy for years after, believing one day I'd hear him whistle. I never did, though.

I called Perk that morning to tell her about the loafers.

"Oh, you were probably sleepwalking and tidying up in your sleep," she said, laughing. "Remember when we were kids and Mama used to go down to the kitchen at midnight and find you sitting at the table, eating cereal? And the next day you would swear you hadn't even woken up the night before?"

"This is different, Perk. Like how Hester would feel Daddy in the house and hear him whistling? She said she could feel the air change. This feels like that."

"You think Daddy moved your shoes?" Perk laughed so hard I could hear Teddy in the background asking her what was funny.

I started pacing my rooms then, through the kitchen and across the living room and out to the sunroom and then back into the guest bedroom and finally my bedroom, a sure sign I was moving from irritated to mad. It's not a large house, but with enough circling you can add up some steps. Listening to Perk's practical explanation made the whole experience sound unreal, and I felt myself losing ground. "No, I'm saying it was strange, is all."

I love my sister, and she has a level head that helps me put most things in perspective, but this wasn't one of those times. This was just another time where if it wasn't based on fact and wasn't right in front of her, plain as day, Perk would toss it aside. I called her on that once when I asked her how she accounted for her faith in God when the only proof we had was from the stories in the Bible. "Faith has nothing to do with fact, Pauline. Faith just is." It made no kind of sense to me that Perk wouldn't believe Hester or me but did believe in God. Perk can always justify her side of an argument, though. She never lets her feelings get in the way, she just states her case and closes it. This was one of those times when feelings and facts just couldn't blend, and we both knew it.

"Well, whoever moved those loafers had the right idea, Pauline. You need to relax and let Mama be. She's got to get used to doing things over there her own way."

We hung up and I continued pacing the rooms. No matter what Perk thought, I knew what I felt. I called Mama. She answered on the fourth ring with the television blasting in the background.

"Hello?"

"Mama, you will never guess."

"Pauline? Where are you? I thought we were going out to lunch," Mama said lightly.

It wasn't even nine-thirty in the morning, but Mama had two speeds, go and go right now.

"Not today Mama. I'll be over later with groceries, but I had to tell you. Remember when Hester used to feel Daddy in the house and hear him whistling?"

Mama laughed then. "She always said he was there looking out for us."

"I think he was, Mama. And last night those loafers of yours moved and I didn't move them. It was the strangest thing, and Perk just laughed it off. I found them this morning under the bed, but when I looked, I felt this love, like there was a presence right there with me."

"A what?"

"A presence, like when Hester felt Daddy in our house. And when I told Perk she told me I was sleepwalking and must have put them under my own bed."

"Well, you used to sleepwalk when you were little, Pauline. After your daddy died. I'd find you down in the kitchen eating at the kitchen table and you didn't remember a thing the next day."

"I know. That's what Perk said too." Up until then I had done a good job of keeping myself from worrying, but I began to feel my neck tightening, already running through the list of what could be causing me to sleepwalk, what terminal condition I might have.

"But it just felt different, Mama. And you used to say you felt Daddy there with us."

"I did. Pauline, if you think something spiritual or magical or whatnot happened, it did. Where do you think faith comes from? Belief is as much experience as it is words. Besides, why care what anybody else thinks about it?"

I could feel my neck starting to loosen, my jaw growing a little slack. It was one thing to have a notion tolerated, and another to have it believed, and quite another to have it accepted even if it wasn't believed. Mama always managed that last one.

"Thanks Mama. I'll bring the groceries after lunch. Love you."

That was a month ago, and the loafers have stayed right where I left them by the front door until this morning. This morning I know right where to look, but I don't look at first. I want to feel this excitement building in me a little longer. And I don't call Perk. I think about calling Mama to tell her, but then decide to just take my cup of coffee and go right back to bed. Something does feel different. Something that is not showing its face just yet but is coming. I turn up the mattress pad to nine and sip my coffee. I picture Hester's face shining, hear her softly saying, "Your Daddy was here, Pauline," long after he had died. I feel a comfort filling me, like someone who loves me is here moving Mama's loafers. A change is coming. Excitement is tingling through me.

3

Choices

IT'S A FEW WEEKS AFTER I FOUND THE LOAFERS a second time under my bed, and I am sitting at my kitchen table reviewing Mama's grocery list when my phone starts ringing. Even before answering I know it must be Perk. Sometimes you know something before it happens, and then it's just the funniest thing once it does. Sure enough, and before I barely say hello, Perk is telling me she and Teddy have missed their flight back from Florida and are stuck at the airport in Miami.

"We're not even sure they have room on the flight tonight," she bubbles, with a spring in her voice that suggests she is more excited than disappointed. "And there is a casino down here that is just more fun than the Fourth of July, and the Cubans, they are everywhere. They are taking your drink order and cashing in your chips, it's like we are in another country. Pauline," she whispers, "missing that flight might just be the best mistake we ever made."

I ask her how much money they lost at the casino, but Perk just keeps talking right over me and starts in on the list of things I will need to take care of.

"Mama has her permanent tomorrow, so be sure to get her there before nine so Janey can get started," she instructs.

"It'll be noon before she's done. And go to my house because the roses need to be watered, and all the ferns."

Perk pauses for a minute and I know she is worrying about what she's left out. Her concern isn't just for how the plants look in the yard, it goes back to Roanoke, where the seeds all came from, and the love Perk has for them. Those plants are as much family heirlooms to Perk as the drop-leaf dining room table from our grandparents' house she and Teddy were given when they married. Each stick of furniture and transplanted fern or rose or poppy seed is as precious as the memories they held. As precious to her as those loafers of Mama's are to me. Perk always calls me the sentimental one, but she can't fool me.

Perk and Teddy have cultivated a backyard full of cinnamon ferns that came from our grandparents' side yard and require almost constant watering in the summer, and a line of pale pink and white rose bushes that came from our grandparents' backyard and now run across Perk and Teddy's front yard. The old-fashioned poppies, from seeds Mama's cousin Babs gave them, are their prizes, planted in patches across the backyard fence line and measuring some years six feet tall, poppies that look like the big salmon colored ones that used to grow up and down the mountains around Roanoke. Two seeds from the same pod can turn out completely different, one streaked with a fiery pink and five feet tall and one a soft salmon color, just as tall, and just as lovely. You don't need to be a botanist to see Mother Nature's aptitude for disparity is one of her constants across the species.

When Perk and I were kids, Babs lived up on Twelve O'clock Knob and grew those poppies everywhere. She'd harvest what she didn't want to winter over and pour the dried seeds into baggies, label each with the year they grew, and store them in her freezer. When Perk and Teddy got married, Babs gave them a big baggy full and told them to tend to those poppies as carefully as they did their marriage. I'm not sure what all has worked with their marriage, but almost fifty years later those poppies at Perk and Teddy's still thrive.

"The poppies," Perk shouts, "oh my goodness I almost forgot the poppies. Be sure to water them in the morning, not the afternoon, and if we aren't back by Saturday touch the seed pods. If they don't spring back, they are ready. I'll call back once we know when we'll be home."

I hang up the phone and look at Mama's grocery list for Kroger's. She won't need a thing for a few days, but I like to stay ahead. McDonald's isn't far from Perk's house, and at the thought of fries and chicken strips my mouth starts watering. I decide to stop by Perk's first and check on the poppies, maybe bring some of those seeds home with me, see what grows.

By the time I get over to Perk's house all I can think about is how hungry I am, so instead of checking the poppies first I go inside to see what food they've left out. I've barely stepped into the hallway when I hear the noise. Low, crackling sounds down in their basement. It sounds like their furnace starting up, but I know that can't be because it is hot as fire outside and the air conditioning is running. My car is the only car out front, so I know it can't be someone coming to visit. Their son James is down in Charlotte and comes home for the holidays and the Superbowl but otherwise stays busy working. The only possibility I can think of is that some rodent has found one of the packed up old boxes Perk keeps down there, the ones filled with her treasures from the Home Shopping Network that never saw the light of day after they got delivered.

I don't like rodents. Even if they were all on an endangered species list, I would let my cats kill the very last one. But I decide catching a rodent can wait until I find a snack. There's nothing on the kitchen counters but a loaf of bread, and the refrigerator comes up fairly empty too, except for a diet lemonade of Teddy's that I know from past experience tastes like cardboard, and some eggs and butter.

I get the eggs scrambling when I hear the crackling sound getting even louder. Whatever rodent is down there, they are not at all shy. I put the bread in the toaster and keep scrambling the eggs, but I am beginning to wonder just how much damage is getting done down in that basement. I have just sat myself down at the table when the basement door slams. It is distinctly that basement door closing hard. I know, because Perk put a bell at the top to remind Teddy to lock the door whenever he comes in from mowing the yard. I am trying to come to terms with how a rodent got that door open as I'm chewing my first bite when it comes to me.

Burglars. I make a dash to the basement steps and holler down just as loud as I can. "Whoever you are," I shout, "I am calling the police." The crackling sound is gone. There's no noise but me breathing hard against the door. It's all I can do to open it and walk down into the darkened basement slowly, still holding a fork full of eggs.

Burglars might like the dark, but I need the light of day, so I march myself back up to the hall to turn the overheads on. Right then I look out the front doorway, still open from when I came in, and see what must be the burglar, a tall boy in a dark hoodie and baggy shorts running across the front lawn, running right over the pink and yellow knock out rose bushes Perk has planted in front of the house. At five foot three, I am a heavy woman and short on legs, but when I see something that needs doing, I get it done. I am out that door and running across that yard waving my fork and shouting, "Stop! Stop that boy!" and make some progress when I see him ahead, down on the ground holding on to an ankle, smeared in soggy mulch Teddy's kept in a pile for the roses.

I run all the way up to him huffing hard and can see he is just a skinny thing, barely old enough for the peach fuzz above his lips. Carrying something that looks an awful lot like the garlic press Perk bought from the HSN. I can't decide whether to poke him with the fork or call his mother. He looks to be in an awful lot of pain.

"Please don't call the police!" The boy is holding his ankle and I see tears welling up in the corners of his eyes. He looks so pitiful I just want to help, and I do, stretching my arm so he can lean against me as he hobbles back to the house, balancing with the help of my one arm, all the while holding the fork and garlic press with my other arm. I can see from first glance that this boy is no thief, he is clean cut, and for a second he reminds me of my nephew, James, back when he was young and peach fuzzed.

James was the sweetest youngster. I would babysit for Perk and Teddy some Friday nights so they could go out and have a date night, back when James was a child. We would have the best time exploring their basement, looking for treasures I would hide ahead of time, toy trains and miniature cars. He would squeal and giggle and run over and hug my neck, saying, "I love you, Aunt Pauline." As he grew, our games changed from treasure hunts to taking imaginary trips to the moon in cardboard boxes Teddy saved from when they had the washer and dryer delivered. James must have been around ten when he handed me a Valentine's card one February and wrote inside, "I am going to marry you, Aunt Pauline."

Later, when he was in high school and growing peach fuzz and playing basketball, I would go with Perk and Teddy to all his games, cheering as loud as anyone there. If I had ever come close to finding a man to have a baby with, I would have wanted to have a child like James. I never did find that man, and I never had a child, but James took hold of my heart and has never let go. Now James is married to Darlene and living in Charlotte, working at one of the banks that keeps changing their name every time they merge and get bigger. Thinking of James even for a second sends a smile to my lips, and I feel a touch of fondness for this boy who reminds me of him.

As I glance over, he looks just pitiful, scared, in pain, and in need of a kind word. I help him limp into the kitchen and take a seat at the table, while I walk over to Perk's refrigerator and pull a bag of frozen peas from the freezer.

"Hold this to your ankle."

The boy nods and extends a long arm towards me.

"Thank-you, ma'am."

"Why in the world would you risk prison for a garlic press?" I blurt it out in a rush. "It makes no kind of sense. Are you on drugs?" I tilt my head and look at him like I am trying to solve a puzzle. Nothing about this boy looks like a thief, not his clean, black hoody with Nike across the front, or his clean baggy shorts or blue tee shirt that looks like it was just washed and pressed.

He scratches his head, his short blonde hair cut within an inch of his scalp, and shakes his head back and forth. "I swear, I just broke in to prove I could do it. That basement door was unlocked too. They said nobody would be home."

"Who said?"

"Just people," he mumbled.

"What people? You spend your life doing stupid things like this you won't have any kind of living ahead of you." I lean over and shake his hood a little to make sure he looks at me.

"You better tell me now if you don't want the police sitting in this house with you and me in the next few minutes. I will call the precinct and tell them in no uncertain terms what you did. Do you hear me?"

The boy looks down and nods his head yes, his bad leg stretched out and propped on a chair, then bends over like he has the world's weight on his shoulders. "Henry and Dan, they dared me to do it, to make me toughen up before I start high school this fall. Ma'am, they have gangs there, and I need to be tough."

"Well, why take a plastic garlic press?"

"It was on top of an open box near the door. I just grabbed the first thing I saw and took off."

He is still bending over, shaking his head, and I can barely make out what he is mumbling. "Do you live around here?"

"Yes ma'am, over on Holsten. I walked over."

"I think my sister knows someone over there, Roberta, Roberta Jackson, I think. Do you know her?"

"No ma'am, but it's a long street."

As I'm watching him holding onto the frozen peas with one hand and brushing his tears with the other, I wonder what kind of world this would be to send a boy to jail for stealing a garlic press.

"What's your name?"

"Sammy Engels."

"Well Sammy, this is my sister Perk's house. My name is Pauline Smith, and when she and her husband Teddy come home, I sure don't want to tell them they were robbed."

I leave him at the table and walk out back, to collect my thoughts and decide what to do with him. While I'm there I collect what dried up seed pods I can find, filling up a baggy with enough poppy seeds to fill my whole backyard. By the time I get back to the kitchen the frozen pea bag is dripping and Sammy's head is almost between his knees. I've already decided not to call the police. He is as helpless as a kitten. I'm about to offer Sammy a ride home when my cell phone rings.

It's Perk. "Change of plans, Pauline." She is practically shouting into the phone, and I can hear music in the background. "We're still at the airport and you are not going to believe it."

"Well, quit shouting," I say. There is just no sense telling her about the burglar right now.

"So here we are sitting in the airport lounge at the bar because all the tables are taken and Teddy's sitting next to this woman. Our flight's already been delayed twice and instead of leaving at five now they're saying it's going to be nine o'clock before we leave. This woman, she looks just like Oprah, Pauline, I kid you not. That's the first thing I say too, you know me, direct as I can be. I lean across Teddy and say, 'Excuse me, are you Oprah Winfrey?' Well she just laughs and shakes her head no and tells me I must be in tune with the universe because as a matter of fact she is a cousin of Oprah's. Can you imagine Pauline? Here we are from Richmond Virginia sitting at an airport bar and talking to Oprah's cousin."

"Perk," I finally get a word in. "What change of plans?"

"Hush your horses, Pauline, I'm fixing to tell you. So, then we find out her name is Rosetta Palmer and she is from Warmly, Pennsylvania and, hold on Pauline. She's a medium."

"A what?" I ask.

"A medium, a fortune teller, a psychic sister, Pauline. That's what she wants us to call her, a psychic sister. And the best part? She thinks we were meant to meet. She told Teddy she must have heard his future self calling to her over the psychic highway, because she only decided to go have a drink at the last minute. She was all set to go to her hotel, but something told her she needed to stop here first. Imagine, Pauline."

I am having a hard time figuring out what this has to do with a change in plans but there is no stopping Perk once she gets started. Poor Sammy is sitting beside me just staring, too. "Hold on Perk," I say, then lean over and whisper. "This is going to take a while, but I can take you home after." He nods and just keeps staring.

"Who are you talking to, Pauline?"

"It's a long story, Perk. What happened to your fortune teller?"

"Psychic sister." Perk starts giggling. "So Rosetta orders us all tequila sunrises and tells us she can read our palms right here right now, but what she is known for back home is her future self-readings where she tells you the psychic address you will live at but don't know yet. And then she gives you the guideposts you'll need to find your psychic address. She tells us it won't cost us a penny even though she usually charges fifty dollars. And Teddy, before I can even agree, pipes in that we are happy to pay for her talent."

I'm about to tell Perk that she's making about as much sense as a nut brain when she says, "So, guess what, Pauline? Rosetta saw long money lines on Teddy's right palm and on my left one! That means we are going to be rich. We are changing our tickets and coming back the day after tomorrow. Rosetta's gone on ahead to the hotel and once we get the tickets we are too. And then we are all going back to the casino. It is meant to be, Pauline. So start picking out your dream vacation because once we hit it big, we'll all go celebrate in style. Oh, and the best part. Rosetta said tonight she's going to give us both psychic address readings at the hotel. I just cannot believe our luck Pauline. I am going to need you checking on the house and watering the poppies, after all. Are you listening Pauline? Pauline?"

"I'm here, Perk." All I can think is that the Florida sunshine must have touched Perk's brain. She is the practical one. Teddy is the gullible one who can get swept up in a soap opera on television and believe what they say is truth. He watches too much of the Fox News too and has more conspiracy theories than either Perk or I can keep up with. But Perk just never falls for far-fetched, and Rosetta is about as far-fetched as they come. It's almost like Perk fell on her head.

I realize I've been staring over at the frozen peas that now are fully melted and dripping on Perk's kitchen floor. Sammy's still holding the bag to his ankle, still staring at me like he's seen a ghost.

"Perk, you be careful at that casino, and don't you head down any psychic highways before telling me first. The funniest thing too, I am sitting right here at your kitchen table and you will not believe what happened to me today."

"Pauline, we got the tickets. Teddy's just walked up and said he's changed the tickets and we're coming back Tuesday night. Wish us luck, Pauline. We'll be coming home with rings on our fingers and bells on our toes and cash to spare. Best part of this trip is going to be the back half."

"Perk, don't spend what you don't have," I say, but she's already hung up. I shake my head, not sure if I am going to worry that Perk's lost her mind or work myself into a temper because she is staying in Florida, leaving me to care for Mama again by myself. I look over at Sammy, still hanging his head like a whipped dog. My stomach is growling and I realize I haven't eaten a thing but a forkful of eggs since morning.

"Sammy," I say, "how about we go on over to McDonald's before I take you home. I have a story to tell you that won't keep, and it will go perfect with chicken strips and fries." Sammy cracks something that is close to a smile, and I take that as a yes.

Sammy has a hard time limping into my car, but after I move the seat all the way back he manages and sits down with a groan.

"I can take you to the doctor if you need me to," I say, hoping the boy will decline the offer. The thought of sitting in an emergency room does not appeal to me one bit.

He does. "No ma'am, it'll be okay."

I reach into my purse and pull out the ibuprofen, hand him two, and say, "This is for when we get to McDonalds. Be sure to eat a little something first, but go on and take them after that. Best to stop that inflammation before it spreads."

"Yes ma'am."

We pull into the McDonalds lot. Sammy hobbles beside me as we walk inside and up to the counter. I know what I want but I look at the board anyway. I like to think it is a courtesy to review the choices somebody took the trouble to list.

I treat us both to chicken strips, fries, and cokes and an apple hand pie for Sammy and take it all back to the table. Sammy is slumping so far down in his seat he almost looks like he's my size. "Sit up, Sammy, this isn't your living room." I put the bag on the table between us and slide into the booth to face him. "Why do you think stealing will make you tough?"

He shrugs. "I guess I don't know. Henry's a year older and he says it does." Sammy looks up at me and then quickly down to the table. If his eyes were drills he would have bored down halfway to China by now.

For all the world I don't think I have seen anybody quite as pitiful as this lanky beanpole of a boy. "Sammy, that is about as ridiculous as my sister thinking a fortune teller is going to change her life." I take a chicken strip and chew. "That's who called me at the house. She's down in Florida talking about fortune tellers and psychic highways." I shake my head. "I'm worried one those flesh-eating amoebae has gotten into her brain." I look down at the plate of chicken strips left on my plate. "This is not like my sister at all." I take another chicken strip and chew. "She does like someone shining a light on her though. When her new Reverend got to town all she could talk about was how impressed she was with him, and she hadn't even heard him preach." I shake my head again, more for myself than Sammy. "I just don't know, but this is not like my sister at all."

Sammy looks up from his food, takes a large slurp from his coke, and smiles. It is the first time I have seen the boy look anything but miserable, and I see, surprisingly, that Sammy has beautiful blue eyes. As sorry as the boy is, he is not unfortunate to look at.

"That's funny," he says.

We eat the rest of the meal in silence. As he is finishing up his hand pie, I make a decision. "Sammy," I say, my voice low so the other customers don't hear, "I want you to promise me something. I want you to go home and tell your mother what you did."

"Mrs. Smith, my mother will kill me. She'll just kill me."

"It's Miss Smith, Sammy. You want to learn to be tough? Face the consequences of the choices you make. There's not a gang at that school tougher than you once you do that."

Sammy looks about as sad as a boy can look. "Yes ma'am."

We are both quiet as I drive down Holsten, the houses brick with wide open porches and swing sets peeking from the backyards. Sammy tells me to stop in front of a long brick ranger about halfway down the street. The lawn is freshly cut and a line of knock out rose bushes bloom on either side of the walkway leading up to the house.

"Well, this is me, thank-you Miss Smith." Sammy opens the door and stretches his bad leg out first, holding the door to steady himself.

"Sammy," I call after him, "I might need my grass cut next year. My regular help is going to college and I am going to need someone. Are you interested?"

Sammy nods yes. I take a pen and a piece of scratch paper from the glove compartment and write down his phone number. As he limps up the walkway, I drive away and head to Kroger's, Mama's grocery list still in the cup holder beside me.

4

Luck

I AM NOT A FANCY WOMAN, I buy the Kroger brand deli meats just like anyone else who isn't a nut brain. And when I ran into Mama's maintenance man Jeremy in the pasta aisle and he looked me up and down, winked, and said, "You are looking fine there, Pauline," I didn't blink. He is a decent enough looking fellow, and lord knows it has been since Clinton's first term—not that almost-president woman Clinton, the other one—that a man looked at me like he was interested. And that was a long-running mistake. Not Clinton, the last time I had a man flirting with me like we were going somewhere.

I was in my forties when Reggie showed up at my door to fix my toilet and ended up asking me on a date. I had gotten a big raise at Blue Cross as a senior processor and was feeling proud. Mama was off on one of her trips with Aunt Eleanor to Germany for Octoberfest, and Teddy, Perk, and James were down in Florida, at Disney World. And I was stuck in Richmond, alone, to celebrate without them. I admit I felt a little lonely, left out. Reggie showed up and swept me off my feet. He talked to me the whole time he was fixing the toilet and then came in to have a cup of coffee with me in the kitchen. Before he handed me the bill, he had asked me out. He took me to the Olive Garden on our first date and the movies on our second and invited himself into my bed on the third date. Even though his kisses were sloppy, the man had a passion that I'd forgotten I could have. By the end of the second month, he had moved in, telling me he loved me and wanted to know everything about me. By then, I was comfortable having him around me, and craving him when he wasn't.

I still drove over to see Mama every few months. Reggie could never go with me. He said he was working whenever I mentioned it, even though I never saw him working any weekends when I wasn't in Roanoke. Perk and I talked on the phone every few days and she would barely ask about Reggie. Perk and Teddy both didn't like him, and that caused a tension between us. They had us over to dinner a few weeks after Reggie and I started dating. Reggie spent the whole evening rolling his eyes at me and ignoring Teddy, who used up most of the dinner conversation telling Reggie about his new idea on an investment to deliver cooked meals to seniors for a monthly fee. James tried to get Reggie to go outside and play catch with him, but Reggie ignored him too.

"Well," Perk said to me after dinner, when I was helping her clean the dishes, "I don't know, Pauline. He sure doesn't look like any plumber I've ever met. His nails aren't even dirty."

"You just don't want me to be happy, Perk. I've finally found someone I love. Be happy for me."

"There is just something off about him, Pauline. Teddy says so too. Have you noticed how often he leaves to use the bathroom whenever we all get together?"

"Good Lord, Perk, maybe he has a small bladder."

Not much gets past Perk, and if I had listened, I might have seen it too. We had been together six months when Reggie asked me for the first loan.

"Sugar, I need to start my own plumbing business. If I can just buy my own tools, I can do it." He had looked at me with those adoring blue eyes shining and I just melted. I wrote him a check that night. Another six months went by and I was letting myself think I had found my forever man; maybe not a Carleton – nobody would ever replace Carleton in my heart – but a man I could love.

And then I came home early from work one Friday and found Reggie sitting at the kitchen table with a bunch of pills sprawled out in little piles. He was trying to gather up all these little bags filled with them when I walked in the kitchen.

"What are you doing home?" I said." And what are you doing with all those pills?"

Reggie jerked his head up, looking at me like I was an intruder, then jumped up and hugged me. "Hey, Sugar. I took off early. You look good enough to eat." Reggie leaned in and started kissing me, but I pushed him back. "C'mon, Sugar, Give me some. These aren't nothing. I promised a friend I would hold on to them while he is in the hospital."

I had been around enough marijuana when I was in high school and college to understand that little bags were for selling, not holding. "Reggie, what are you doing selling pills?"

"Sugar, I am not selling pills. I told you. Hey, listen, I have a surprise." He pulled out an envelope with two plane tickets inside from his back pocket and waved it in front of me. "Fort Lauderdale, Sugar. This weekend. I got us a room on the beach, too." Reggie leaned back in and this time I did let him kiss me. He could sweet talk me out of any fight we might have. He stuffed all the little bags into a grocery sack and promised me he was taking them back to his friend. "I don't want you worrying, Pauline."

I did worry, but I didn't say a thing to Perk. I didn't want her to be right about Reggie, and I sure didn't want to see the look on her face that said I told you so. I wanted to believe Reggie. That weekend I flew in a plane for the first time, drank pina coladas on the beach, and listened to Reggie talk about his dreams for us. I felt closer to him than I ever had and hung on to every word he said. We got back to Richmond late on Sunday night, and by the time we picked up our suitcase and drove home, I was dead tired. I had work the next morning. As we walked in the house, Reggie turned to me and said, "Oh, Sugar, I forgot. I have a big job in the morning, and I need to buy some more tools. Can you loan me another thousand?"

I had never seen any new tools. The only plumbing supplies I ever saw Reggie bring home fit in a tote bag. I was too tired to think, much less question Reggie about anything. "I guess," I said.

"I'll be gone before you wake up. Could you write it now?"

Reggie was gone the next morning, and when I got back from work he was still gone. I cooked our dinner and waited, but Reggie didn't show. I called Perk and told her about Fort Lauderdale, and how much fun we had, but there was something empty in my voice, something even Perk could hear.

"What's wrong?" she said. "You sound weird. Are you sick?"

"No. I don't know, Perk. Reggie isn't home. He told me he had to leave early for a job, but I don't know. Something's not right."

"Oh, Pauline, trust your gut. Something is not right with him. No decent man asks you for money and then doesn't mention paying you back."

"He did it again last night, Perk. He borrowed another thousand dollars. He'll pay me back."

"Well, we'll see."

Perk and I hung up and I waited. And waited. Reggie never came home. A week later Perk called and told me she had read in the paper about a drug bust, an operation illegally selling prescription pain medication up and down the East Coast, from Fort Lauderdale to New York City. Reggie was listed as one of the people arrested.

At any rate, Jeremy and Reggie both had that same gleam in their eyes, mischief. Turned out Reggie's mischief was illegal, so when it dawns on me that Jeremy is flirting, all I can think about is Reggie. Alarm bells start ringing in my head and I freeze up like a deer in headlights. I don't even pick up my angel hair for marinara Wednesday, just wish him a good day and start back over to the checkout.

It's not like I don't have men in my life. I am not a desperate woman. The mailman Robert Redford (I am still dumb struck his Mama named him that), he goes by Bob, stops by almost every day to hand deliver my mail. I've started to think Bob is flirting when he knocks on the door with my magazines and bills and social security checks and then hands them to me with a smile. He's awfully slow to ask me out. He's been on my delivery route for months now, but I've decided that's part of his kindness, taking things slow, nothing more. Bob is newly divorced and from South Hill, two things he volunteered shortly after introducing himself to me. I do like to call him by his full name every now and then to hear it out loud: Robert Redford.

Nobody would ever call Bob a pretty man, and the truth is he has a worn look to him, like a hound run too long on a hunt. There is something, though, in the way his brown eyes light up when he sees me and how close he leans in when he talks to me. I find myself catching my breath whenever he comes close, stirring parts of me left dusty over the years, pleasures long forgotten.

The first day he delivered the mail I was coming out the front door as he was walking up with my mail.

"Mrs. Smith?" he said, smiling.

"Miss Smith, but Pauline is just fine," I said, smiling back.

"Well, it sure is nice to meet you, Pauline. I took over the route for Barry, so I'll be by with your mail daily." He leaned back like he was practically sitting on his haunches. I felt a stirring inside me, the look of him all at once familiar and fascinating. I shook that feeling right off. I was already late getting to Mama's, so I just waved and kept walking. There was a little spring to my step though, and as the days went by and Bob started knocking on the door and chatting as he handed me my mail, I began to feel a lightness like a smile was growing inside me.

Bob caught me off guard one day when he stopped by and handed me my social security check. "Pauline, if you don't mind me saying, you sure brighten my day." Bob leaned halfway through my open doorway then, grinning.

"Well, aren't you something." I laughed, and my heart started singing just a little.

One day not long after he took the route, Bob came up to my door and knocked. I had been in the kitchen, putting up groceries. By the time I got to the front door, he was halfway around my house.

"Bob?" I'd said, a little confused why he was headed to my backyard.

"Pauline! I knocked but when you didn't answer the door I got a little worried." Bob smiled then and practically bounced across the yard and up onto my stoop. "I wanted to make sure you saw your social security check was here."

He leaned in so far our noses were practically touching and handed me the envelope. "I know how we all need our steady income," he said, grinning wide and twinkling those brown eyes as bright as a light bulb switched on.

"That is real sweet, Bob, and even though I am fortunate to have more than just this old check to rely on, every penny counts, doesn't it?" I smiled then and thought Bob might just be the nicest man I had ever met. Bob turned away to leave and as he was walking to the sidewalk, I had called out. "Hey, Bob."

He turned around and was about to walk right back, when I waved him off and said, "You know, you brighten my day every day."

We both smiled then for so long I thought my breath was going to just seize up, but then he had turned and walked back out to the sidewalk. It's a funny thing how a heart can be starving after it's broken in two and then fade so far from your thinking you forget what it is that's beating. And then someone comes along and just like that, every beat is a joy. I had just about decided Bob was that.

Love has a funny way of waking up the parts of you that you hadn't known were there. And the memory of that first time holds to you like a skin, no matter how old you get to be. I turned sixteen in the early seventies, wearing bell-bottomed jeans and peasant blouses and growing out my hair down my back and clinging tight to an anger I'd carried since childhood. It was a good time to be an outsider. The whole world seemed to be protesting the Vietnam War and the establishment. All those walls I put up after Daddy died turned to cement, and the deeper I buried my grief, the angrier I became on the surface.

By the time I started high school, I had found a place to point my anger. I was a freshman the year Perk was a senior,

and along with resenting her for taking trips with Mama to visit colleges and leaving me with Granny (even though when invited I had refused to go with them), I decided Mama was to blame for Daddy dying. If she hadn't married a man who was going to die, my life would have been normal. I pointed all the anger brewing inside me at the both of them.

Perk was accepted at Virginia Commonwealth University early decision that fall, and we celebrated with Granny at the Roanoker Restaurant. That morning, I had drawn an X in magic marker on the front of her favorite blouse earlier in the day.

"Pauline, you psycho. Why did you do this?" she had said when she walked into her closet to hang up a sweater that afternoon. I had left the top in full view for her to see when she walked in.

"I am not dumb, Perk. You called me a moron."

"I said you were a moron for not telling Mama you need help with math. She can get you a tutor."

"I don't need help."

"Great, then you are a moron for not admitting you need help. You might as well join the army. You're never going to get into college."

When Mama got home from showing houses, Perk was at the door, showing her the top.

"Pauline." Mama's voice was clipped and hard. "Come down here right now."

I slumped down the stairs slowly, but she was standing at the bottom, watching me.

"Why did you ruin your sister's top?"

"I don't know. She made me mad."

"Have you lost your mind? We do not destroy property. If you are mad at your sister, talk to her. Look at me, Pauline."

I was still sitting halfway down the stairs, looking at the light green carpet.

"You will rake the leaves this Saturday and do the laundry all week. No television. Perk, I'll take you to the mall Saturday and buy you another top."

Perk had hugged Mama and thanked her and walked right past me on the stairs, not saying a word. She didn't say another word to me until we were at the restaurant.

Halfway through the meatloaf special, Perk said, "And Pauline thinks she is going to be a veterinarian, Granny, and she can't even understand math." Perk had looked over at me, sneering.

"Shut up." I leaned over the table for effect and said it again, "Just shut up, Perk."

"Both of you, shut up." Granny said. "Your mother is trying to do something nice and here you are fighting like cats and dogs."

"Listen to your grandmother," Mama said.

Granny and Mama spent the rest of the meal talking about the real estate market and the houses Mama was showing. Perk and I didn't look at each other until we were leaving. We rolled our eyes at the same time when Granny stood at the cashier counter chatting with a woman for so long Mama had to coax her to wrap it up so we could leave.

I ended up failing geometry. Mama found me a tutor over the summer, and every Wednesday for two hours I had to sit at our kitchen table and study equations with a woman who would lean over the table and ask, "Do you see, do you see?" By the time I took geometry for a second time in my sophomore year, I passed with a B. I started concentrating more on the homework. The last thing I wanted was another tutor staring at me across our kitchen table.

Perk was declaring a major in economics at Virginia Commonwealth when I started junior year. I signed up for the basketball team try-outs that year because the other girls on my block were trying out, then quit before I was called to try-outs.

"Why did you quit?" Mama asked over dinner one night.

"Because I don't want to. I don't know. I just did."

"Pauline, you can't go through life just quitting things. And if you don't know why you are doing something, don't do it."

"Well, I know. I'm too short for the basketball team."

Mama shook her head but didn't say a thing more.

The house seemed to fill with my run-ins with Mama. Without Perk home to distract me or diffuse our arguments, I butted heads with Mama almost daily. I would put on my blue jeans and peasant blouse and go down for breakfast already knowing what Mama would say. "You're wearing that to school?" Even though Mama pretty much let me pick my outfits for school, she never hesitated to tell me what she thought. As much as I wanted to be the outsider, Mama's opinion mattered to me, and I would hear the criticism in her voice and cringe inside, holding in my hurt feelings and covering them all up with my anger.

She drew the line when it came to going to church though, and when Mama drew the line, there was no crossing it.

"When you are in the house of the Lord, you will dress with respect."

"I need to express who I am, Mama."

"While you are living in my house, Pauline, you will wear decent clothes to church."

I stopped arguing about what to wear to church, but we fought every Sunday morning about whether or not I would go at all. In the end, I always did.

Mama insisted we eat at the kitchen table together every evening. She would heat up the pot roast Hester had made over the stovetop and ask how my day had been. I held back much of what my days included, but the politics of the war were being talked about everywhere back then. Walter Cronkite talked about the latest protests and the death counts in Vietnam on the six o' clock news, while the kids at school in bell-bottomed jeans huddled together between classes and ranted about Nixon's refusal to end the draft, end the war. Kids talked about their brothers, the ones in Vietnam, some already dead, and called Nixon the evil one. Their anger was contagious, and I found myself ranting right along with them.

One night, over pork chops and fried potatoes, I struck up a conversation I decided we needed to have. This was election year and I was stirred up. Nixon had to go. "Mama, why are you a Republican? Don't you know Nixon is forcing teenagers to go to war?"

"I am not a Republican, Pauline. I voted Republican during the last election, but I also voted Democrat when John Kennedy was running. I am an Independent."

"Well, that's worse. It means you can't make up your mind."

Mama turned from the stove and studied me for a second. "Have you ever known me not to know my mind? I look at the candidate, not the party, study his policies, his convictions."

"Then vote for McGovern. He wants to end the war, do away with the draft, and provide income to poor people."

"Those are all good policies, Pauline. And I will consider them when I do vote in November. I'll consider both of the candidates' policies."

"But Nixon is evil. One of the kids at school said we do not know the half of what he's been up to since he was elected.

She has a boyfriend who was drafted, and she hasn't heard from him in months."

"I am sorry about your friend's boyfriend, Pauline. I'll pray he comes home safely. But you can't base your opinions on hearsay."

"Nixon put us in Vietnam and nobody wants us there, Mama."

"Is that what they are saying these days? Honey, that war started long before he came into office."

"Well, you don't have a son being drafted."

"No, but your Grandaddy was in two wars and your Daddy earned a silver medal saving his crew from sinking in the Pacific. He had nightmares, Pauline. It was no picnic, but he came home proud to serve, proud to protect his country."

"Mama, what if I was sent over there? McGovern wouldn't send me. And Nixon isn't interested in me, much less trying to help the poor people."

"He may not be a great president, but I am Independent. And I wait until election day to make up my mind."

"Well, that is just your privilege talking."

"My what?"

"Privilege, Mama. If you were poor, you would see the Democrats do more for poor people."

"Pauline, you come from privilege. Hard-earned privilege. Grandaddy worked hard and used his privilege as service to others. Do you think all of his patients paid him? They didn't, but he never complained. He treated all his patients the same. Besides, there is nothing wrong with working hard and earning a living. We are blessed to have the good fortune to earn a good living and be good stewards of our wealth. You should be grateful."

"Well, I want better lives for the poor people. There is no justice in some people starving while others are sitting pretty.

What about the growing divide in this country between the haves and the have nots? Just look at all the people coming to the church food pantry. We need to help them."

"We all want that, Pauline. And the good Lord knows we all should want to lift up all souls, not just some. But no matter how you want to dress, you are my daughter and you need to accept that the family who loves you also has privilege."

"But we have to do something about it. I want to do something about it, Mama. I want you to do something about it."

"Then go study that, learn how you can help those people, Pauline. But quit wasting your time trying to get me to do it for you. My choices are my own, and your choices are all yours. And you are old enough to see that."

During that junior year, all my childhood friends looked happy and normal, and talked about their boyfriends and their new outfits, wearing signet rings and going to football games with boys who wore upturned collars and lettered jackets. I felt anything but happy or normal. All Margaret talked about was the football player she was dating. We didn't have much in common aside from picking a college. I felt like I was on the outside of myself, and as alone as I had ever felt. I started to gravitate to those kids Mama would call troublemakers, spent the minutes between classes on the smoking block, hanging out with people who didn't know a thing about my Daddy dying.

They all looked as unhappy and angry as I did. I didn't smoke cigarettes or marijuana or even drink beer, but I would nod and smile whenever anyone talked about getting high. I usually sat next to a girl named Melanie and listened to her talk about her crazy mother. Her stories were so foreign to the childhood I'd had, it was a relief to escape my own life and hear about hers.

"My damn mother went out and wrecked the car last night. Hit a parked car after being at the bar with her boyfriend and took off before the cops could come. Then this morning the cops show up at our door and arrest her for hit and run." Melanie had glanced at me and must have noticed my wide-eyed deer-in-the-headlights look, and said, "Hey, you wanna get high today?"

"I guess." I didn't know what else to say.

It was Friday and the last class had been cancelled so everybody could go to the gym for a pep rally. Melanie and I slipped behind the gym and down into the alley behind the school. I took one puff and Melanie shouted, "No, not like that," and proceeded to inhale the joint and just stand there holding her breath, before letting out a long line of smoke. She passed the joint and I took a long inhale. I didn't take a second one, I was already feeling light and silly.

That day I rode the bus home smiling, and when Mama saw me come in the door, she asked, "What happened to you?"

"Can't I be in a good mood?" I stomped up to my bedroom and shut the door. Mama was working a lot selling real estate then, but she was always home when I got back from school.

"I've got to go back to the office. Hester made lasagna." She stood at my bedroom door. "Love you," she added, before going back downstairs and out the door.

I liked the way pot made me feel, and I spent more and more time after school with Melanie and her friends, smoking and listening to Bob Dylan and Joni Mitchell. Eventually, I learned to like the taste of beer as well. The times they were a-changing, we all sang at the tops of our lungs, while Mama sold real estate and I made up excuses for coming home later and later.

Carleton transferred to our high school that year, moving down off Catawba mountain after his parents divorced. He caught me by surprise. I was so busy burying feelings and keeping my heart locked tight, you could have knocked me over with a feather the first time that boy smiled at me, smiled with his whole self, it felt like. He walked up to me on the smoking block, grinning as he offered me a Winston, and I felt a surprising flutter like a bird taking wing. Those songs do not get it wrong. Sometimes it just takes one look.

Carleton was an outsider too. There is no kind of sense to anyone saying the children of divorced parents or the children of dead parents are all going to act the same and need the same things to get through pain. Perk and I prove that point. She went through the years after Daddy died spilling tears and talking about her feelings, crying over Shirley Temple movies and rainy days, cleaning out all that sadness with hugs from Mama and her friends, seeking comfort from her pain, and keeping her heart open to whoever happened her way. When she met Teddy their freshman year at Virginia Commonwealth University, her heart was a big old welcome sign. And Teddy's was too. All the while I was wearing clothes that stamped me an outsider and drifting through my days, numbing myself with beer and marijuana, Perk and Teddy were falling in love. Making future plans.

Carleton had four brothers, but he was the only one of them who took his parents' divorce personally. He made a point of finding trouble and trying to numb the anger inside him. He walked up to me on the smoking block that day and I think we both just recognized ourselves in each other, drawing us together in a powerful way. That boy was the only person who didn't make me feel like I was split in two. I loved him in a way I couldn't control and didn't want to. He was my best friend, my future. We would join the other students hanging at the smoking block after school to protest the war, carrying our signs downtown and driving over to Roanoke College for anti-war rallies, showing out all our anger for the cause. Carleton and I would drive home in his Camaro after those rallies and talk about where we would travel after he finished airplane mechanic school and I graduated from college. We decided we would go to Mexico first and buy the good marijuana, maybe buy a van and travel through Central America, too.

Carleton was not what I would call a self-aware boy, but when we were together, mostly spending our days after school sitting on the hood of his old Camaro, looking out on the Blue Ridge Parkway, listening to Traffic or Jimi Hendrix on the eight track tape blasting from under the dash, passing a bottle of Rolling Rock back and forth, I felt a comfort filling me that was the closest I ever got to holding my Daddy's hand and walking up the trails on Yellow Mountain before he got sick, the comfort of trusting, no matter what is up ahead. While those mountains in the distance edged in blue hid the sun setting, we would sit quiet. Something about sitting quiet with Carleton drew me closer to him, like we shared something no one else had.

Carleton was the first boy I ever kissed. Before then, I just didn't see the point, and if a boy liked me, I made sure with a look that he knew I did not feel the same. Carleton kissed me for the first time in the high school parking lot one day after school. He leaned over and took my hand and kissed me soft and then worked his tongue deep inside my mouth and kept moving it side to side until I felt like I was about to explode. The desire I felt so low and strong was shocking to me. I pulled back and told him I was not having sex until I graduated. Carleton, sweet as ever, grinned and said, "Well, there is a lot we can do before then."

Carleton taught me all the ways to make love without having sex, and I thrilled with the desire it brought on. The need for Carleton's touch clawed at me and brought me all the closer to him. Weekend nights I'd tell Mama we were going to the football game or the pep rally or the basketball game, and Carleton and I would find a parking lot, an overlook, or an alleyway, and roll around the backseat of that Camaro, giggling and stroking each other and carrying on. He never argued about us not having sex, even though I knew he'd had a girlfriend up on Catawba, and I'd heard rumors that she had gone all the way with him. On the days he was working at the Esso station pumping gas and cleaning windows, I stayed home and studied, mostly just doodling in a notebook and writing in my journal, studying just enough to get B's in all my classes.

Nobody would have called him handsome, but Carleton had the softest lips and the bluest eyes that looked for all the world like he was carrying the biggest secret and just couldn't wait to tell you. His long black hair down to his shoulders would shake all over his face when he laughed. And we laughed a lot.

Perk was in her senior year at college, and Mama was spending her days showing houses to new doctors at the hospital and to the children of her friends moving back to Roanoke to buy their first homes. Mama stayed busy and didn't say too much about Carleton and I spending most of our time together. I think she was downright relieved I had a friend. I never heard her complain about his long hair or ripped up blue jeans. She did enough of that complaining about what I wore. Deep down, I think Mama knew how important he was to me. She would make sure Carleton ate dinner with us once a week, quiz him on his goals, how his Mama was doing, and Carleton was always polite, sweet-talking her about her cooking. He told Mama before I knew a thing that he planned to go to machinery school in Lynchburg after graduation. Carleton wanted to be an airplane mechanic. Mama said that sounded wonderful. Before I knew it the two of them were thick as thieves.

Carleton was not what I would call a walking mistake, but he sure had bad luck. On the day we were set to graduate he decided to drive his Camaro up on the parkway, on a pretty June day when the mountains were green and the rhododendron was blooming and blackberry blossoms were sparkling white all up and down the ridges. Somewhere around the S curve above McAfee's Knob, Carleton lost control of that Camaro he had worked so hard to keep running. We never found out what got in his way, or if nothing did, but the skid marks showed him doing a half circle before the car flipped and tumbled all the way done into a gully, way below the road.

Perk was already home from college and planning her wedding to Teddy. She was sitting beside Mama and Teddy and Granny at my high school graduation when I walked across the stage. Grandaddy had died years ago or else he would've been right there beside Granny. None of us knew right then that Carleton was dead in a gully off the side of a no-name mountain at mile marker 809 on the Blue Ridge Parkway. When the principal called his name and he didn't show, no one thought much of it. Just Carleton skipping out on another school function. I felt a twinge of anger, though, that he hadn't told me he was skipping graduation. The rest of our class of '72 threw our caps and hugged each other and firmed up plans for the parties that night. Mama drove us all in Granny's Cadillac over to the Roanoker Restaurant for a celebration dinner, me with not a care in the world other than when I could get away and go find Carleton. The phone rang after we got home from dinner, while I was changing to go out to the graduation parties.

It is fair to say I split back in two after Carleton died. I followed Perk and Teddy to Richmond and college and a dormitory and a life of getting just close enough to friends for them to like me and never close enough to trust them with my feelings. I chose social work for my major and after the one mandatory psychology class decided I would work with emotionally disturbed adolescents. Finally, I thought I had found something I could relate to. If anyone knew what it meant to be an emotionally disturbed teenager, it was me. As long as I could help someone else, I didn't have to think too hard about myself.

A boy in my Statistics class freshman year asked me out and we ended up in his dorm room having sex with David Bowie's song 'Starman' blasting down the hallway. The whole time the boy was sweating and thrusting his penis inside me, all I could think about was Carleton, how we had planned our first time, after graduation, to be in a Holiday Inn room with candles on the table and sipping Blue Nun from plastic cups. Laying instead with this boy, after, on his single bed, face to face, hearing him say, "thank-you", and me saying "your welcome," my life felt as disconnected from reality as a balloon floating over a line of trees.

I graduated college with a degree in Social Work and started work at the Blue Cross Blue Shield three bus stops from my apartment on Monument Avenue. At first I thought that was a temporary job, until I could find a job in social work, but the days turned to months. And between the benefits and the salary I started liking the comfort of having that job, knowing how to do the work, which was claims processing all of their major medical claims. Saving the world lost its luster, and so did I. I hung up the peasant blouses and bell-bottomed jeans and bought business suits and business casual slacks and tops at Steinmart's on Broad Street, and I went shopping with Mama and Perk when she would come visit. She always found me the perfect shoes at Saxon's to go with all the work outfits. I adopted a kitten from the animal shelter and named her Trixie and started reading best-selling mysteries, James Patterson and Sue Grafton my favorites.

There wasn't much fun in my life other than stepping out with some of my women co-workers from time to time, going to O'Charley's for a Friday happy hour, or Olive Garden for the birthday lunches. The girl who sat in the cube next to me liked to go to the movies on Saturdays and invited me to tag along. Ginny had a boyfriend in the Navy and didn't get to see him much. We spent a lot of Saturdays watching the new releases. Time moves on whether you are having fun or not.

I spent the rest of my twenties and thirties dating young men who liked me and letting them go once I started feeling something for them, or else liking the young men who didn't care two cents for me and watching them turn away. I was drawn to the boys who were going to cause me pain. All the while I was learning to live on my own in Richmond, and Perk and Teddy were living in their honeymoon years, Mama was seeing the world, traveling with Aunt Eleanor to Spain and Majorca and England and France, bringing home gifts to Perk and me and writing us postcards.

She travelled more in the years after Perk and I moved to Richmond than she had in her whole life before then. She and her friends the Richardsons, a painter and his wife, travelled to Holland so he could paint the windmills, and then went back the next year so he could paint the tulips. Mama was forever buying his paintings and hanging them in her living room. She would ask me sometimes if I wanted to come along on one of her trips, but I never did. I just didn't see us traveling together. I wanted to travel, to some warm island far away from everywhere. Carleton and I had talked about going to Bali one day. But traveling with Mama just didn't sound like fun. By then I felt about as separate from Mama as I ever had, drifting farther from who I thought she wanted me to be and pointing my anger at times at her.

Perk and Teddy had bought their first home by then and didn't live but a few miles away. Holidays we all spent in Roanoke, and a good many weekends too. I'd pack Trixie in her carrier and drive to Roanoke, bringing Mama her favorite chocolates from the candy store down on Cary Street. I never did bring another boyfriend home after Carleton. She'd ask if I was seeing someone, and I'd always say, "No one special."

I start fixing the red sauce I'm making for Marinara Wednesday, knowing good and well I'll have to stop back at Kroger for the angel hair I didn't buy. Jeremy is still clouding my mind, and for the tiniest minute I feel a twinge guilty, like I am two-timing Bob—a feeling as foreign to me as speaking Russian. I've dated some, but I've never looked at one man with any interest while seeing another. Besides, Bob is just a friend and Jeremy is at best an acquaintance. I laugh at my foolishness and stir the sauce.

The years since my last boyfriend have stretched into decades. I was in my forties when I met Reggie (that was when Clinton was in office the first time), and I had already bought my house and had money left over after bills and a mortgage. Sometimes the heart just waits and waits and then, for no reason at all it opens up and lets in the first person it sees. That was what it seemed like with Reggie. I had not been looking, hadn't even thought of being with a man before he came walking up to my front door.

Reggie was not much to look at, but he did have these blue eyes that lit up like you were the most important person in the world when he was looking at you. I remember our first date at Olive Garden, how he leaned across the table and looked at me with those eyes and told me I was the prettiest woman in the world. Turned out he looked that way at a lot of women, but I didn't find that out until after I had lent him most of my savings. Perk always said I was one of the lucky ones though. He got arrested for selling pills to an undercover agent before I had put him on the deed to the house. Love is like that sometimes, when all you want is for it to work and then it doesn't, there does seem to be a silver lining.

It would be fair to say I've never had much luck in love. Not like Perk and Teddy, married these past fifty years and going strong. Or Mama and Daddy, even though Daddy died too young and Mama decided one love was enough to last her a lifetime. I have had my tries at love though, and just because none of them took doesn't mean I haven't been living alone just fine. A house I call home and my cats to keep me warm, and family. I tell myself this whenever I feel a pang of loneliness taking hold. Lately, that's been less and less. If truth is being told, having Bob stop by every day has become part of a routine I look forward to.

I give the red sauce a stir and decide to sprinkle in some extra garlic pieces I've chopped up and left on the kitchen counter. I can take it or leave it, but I remember Bob telling me once he loved a good red sauce with lots of garlic in it. It's funny what you remember a person saying long after they said it. Bob has started delivering my mail later and later in the afternoon. I might just ask him to step in for a plate one of these days soon. Could be Bob is waiting on me to make the first move.

I've put the lid back on and set the burner to simmer when the phone rings. I catch it on the second ring and say, "Hello?" I wait, sometimes it takes Mama a breath to speak up and Perk can be in the middle of doing something else when she calls and take even longer.

There is only silence on the other end of the phone. I speak louder. "Hello." There have already been a few calls this month where no one talked, pranking teenagers, I have guessed, but now I am getting fed up. I hang up and turn back to the stove.

The phone rings again. I am ready to tell whoever is pranking me where to go, but when I say hello this time, it's Perk who speaks up.

"Pauline," she says, "you will not believe this but those people running Mama's senior solutions complex called me all the way down here in Florida. If I hadn't thought it was an emergency I never would have answered."

"Well you know you are first on their call sheet," I say.

"They were not at all nice. You cannot even imagine all the problems those people try to stir up to get us to pay them more money. And this time they tell me there have been complaints about Mama walking in the hallways in just her nightgown and slippers. And I know as well as you do Mama never even gets out of bed without putting on that old housecoat over her nightgown."

"Did you tell them that?" I ask, opening the lid and stirring the sauce again to keep it thickening.

"Of course I did. I told that woman Mama is more active than half those folks living there and at 96 she's older than all of them. Pauline, I will tell you what, when I told that woman if they didn't like Mama living there we would move her elsewhere, she shut right up. All she wanted was to get us to pay them more money to look in on Mama. Don't answer if that woman tries calling you. It was that supervisor, Laura."

"I won't," I say just as Perk hangs up.

I spoon up the sauce to see if it is coming together, inhale the aroma of red sauce, and hear someone knocking at the front door.

"Pauline, Pauline are you there?" Bob calls out.

I feel downright giddy as I call out, "Coming, Bob."

There is something about giddiness that overpowers any other feeling you might have. As I walk up to my door and glance over at the loafers, lined up beside the doorway, and sense the glow of light on them out of the corner of my eye, I don't even take time to pause. Bob is on the other side of that door and I can't wait to see him. Feeling this giddy is as good as being wrapped up in a giant hug.

I open the front door smiling. "Well I was about to call the branch, you're so late. I was beginning to think you'd already come by while I was at Kroger's." I keep smiling but can't help but notice Bob's shirt is wrinkled, and he looks like he hasn't shaved today.

"Pauline, well it's been a day." Bob shakes his head and hands me my Southern Living magazine. "But I wanted to make sure you were all right, Pauline. Besides, isn't it time for that social security check?"

I decide right then Bob is the most considerate man I have ever met. I can feel my face heating up as I hold his gaze and smile. "Oh, I am always alright, Bob, but it sure is nice to see you."

"But that check comes every third Tuesday, doesn't it Pauline? And I looked over the block's mail and didn't see it. A few of the mail sorters at the main branch were fired for stealing mail."

"Oh my goodness, that is terrible, Bob. It's a good thing Teddy talked me into switching to direct deposit for my monthly checks, even the social security."

"Oh." Bob looks away.

I feel a thrill lighting me and think, why, Bob must be a shy man. I can still feel the heat on my face. I have never figured out how these kind of moments can feel brand new even when you get to be as old as me. I suppose if love springs eternal, then feeling giddy does too. The feeling is as good as one of those energy drinks Teddy keeps promoting to Perk and me, and I blurt out before I can catch myself.

"I am making a red sauce but I'm out of noodles. How about a cup of coffee?"

"It has been a day and that sounds good." Bob smiles again, but he isn't leaning in like he always does, and he looks a little sheepish, like he's been caught with a hand in the cookie jar. I am not someone who tries to make a body feel self-conscious though, and so I smile a little wider.

"Come on in," I say.

Bob follows me back to the kitchen and it feels as familiar to listen to his footsteps behind me as it does to wake up to a sunrise, known and surprising at the same time.

I brew a fresh pot of coffee as Bob makes himself at home at the table, stretching his long legs underneath the table and sitting down low in his seat. I keep standing at the counter beside the coffee pot, nervous all of a sudden to be so close to Bob. Perk has always been the one to do the small talk, and the longer I stand at the counter the more it dawns on me that Bob is not saying one word, just looking down at the table and tapping his fingers every so often.

Almost as if he had read my thoughts, Bob looks up, smiles at me, and says "that coffee smells about as good as my Mama's used to be, Pauline. And after a day like this, I can't think of a thing better."

I look over at Bob and hold my tongue because at any moment I know I am going to ask him what in the world has happened today, blurt it out with no grace whatsoever, just ask him in my hungry voice like I do when Perk is holding something back from me. Without him offering up any part of the story. All of a sudden I want to know a lot more about Bob, what he likes for dinner, where he goes in his free time, and I especially want to know what happened to him today. The thought of needing more churns my stomach, but I don't let it show.

The coffee pot heaves a final sputter and I turn to fill our cups before I unfurl a thousand questions. The red sauce has already filled the room with smells of fresh summer tomatoes and basil cooked for hours down low. Bob glances over at his watch a few times and apologizes each time he does it.

"It's not the company, Pauline. And this might be the best coffee I've ever had, and that's saying a lot." Bob's brown eyes are twinkling again, and he is sitting up straight, looking lighter in his seat.

"Oh I know, Bob. I'm real happy you could stop by at all." I smile and hold his gaze a little long. I am feeling bolder by the minute, and that surprises me more than just about anything. My words asking Bob over for dinner are on the tip of my tongue struggling to find their way, but something is holding them in. My boldness starts to disappear, and I let it.

After we've both finished our coffee, Bob gets up and takes both our cups over to the sink, and begins washing them. I jump up and our hands brush as I reach over and take a cup from him, and the shiver I feel is downright pleasure.

"Oh no, Bob, you are still working. These will keep."

Bob nods and walks over to the mail bag he's left in the corner. "Thank you, Pauline. You've just about turned around what was an awful day." He picks up the bag and makes his way out to the front door.

I follow Bob and wave good-bye as he leaves, then close the door behind him. I'm already thinking about when I'll ask Bob to stay for Marinara Wednesday dinner, beating myself up just a little for not doing it today. I sigh, feeling like a teenage girl, and glance down at the spot where my loafers should be, and are not.

I am still thinking about how much I like Bob's smile as I walk back to the bedroom and look under my bed, not for a minute afraid or suspicious. The current is already pulsing through me, calling me to exactly where I need to be. A rush of coolness brushes my face as I lie down on my side. My arm reaches in and sweeps across the floor and with my cheek pressing down against the scatter rug, I see the loafers, tucked away at the far edge of the headboard, and I sense them glowing with a light that twinkles and calls me, washing me with love. As I stretch my arm over to reach them, I feel a warmth rushing over me. For the longest time I don't want to move or hardly even breathe. I haven't been to church since I moved to Richmond all those years ago, but you don't forget that washing of the spirit you feel when someone sings a beautiful hymn or a minister speaks directly to your pain and fills your heart. Not like the brush of a man's hand, something deeper. This is like that, and it doesn't matter who else believes it. Like Mama said, if you believe it is spiritual or magic or whatever, it is. I pull the loafers out, slip them on my feet, and proceed back to the kitchen to put up the sauce. Some things just don't have names.

5

How Did We Get Here

"I WAS JUST MAD AS HOPS," Perk says. It's two days since Bob's coffee visit, and I am driving her and Teddy home from the airport. "You would have thought that woman stepped right out of heaven's gate and handed me and Teddy the keys to the kingdom, for all her talk. And there we were, sitting in the back of a cab in Miami Florida driving to a converted Pizza Hut Rosetta called the psychic Highway Rest Stop, and all I can think is, How did we get here?"

"It's a question," I say.

"Pauline, do not, do not ever listen to someone telling you who you are, who you are going to be." Perk is leaning in so close she is almost holding the steering wheel. "That woman charged us fifty dollars apiece to read our palms and then had the nerve to tell Teddy his aura was in disrepair. Who even does that? We were sitting in the back of that cab, after we had lost most of our money, and Rosetta had already read our palms and collected our cash, and here she is telling poor Teddy his aura needs fixing." Perk stares out the window for a minute and then goes back to the story.

"And that's when I nudged Teddy, but you know Teddy, you have to look him square in the face and hit him with a baseball bat to get his attention once he is on a roll. And we just kept driving to who knows where and that meter keeps running up the money and Teddy and me and Rosetta are somewhere in South Miami and I don't think they even speak English there. I have never seen so many Nail Salons and boarded up Blockbusters and Massage Parlors and broken-down gas stations in my life, Pauline. And then Rosetta points to this Pizza Hut sign and there is a banner across the front door that says Psychic Highway Rest Stop and she tells the cab driver to stop."

"Perk," I say as we are pulling into their driveway, "there is something you should know about the house."

"It can keep, Pauline, I have not used a bathroom since Miami."

Before Teddy has even unfastened his seatbelt, Perk is out of the car and up the front steps. I can hear her muttering about the broken rose branch as she disappears into the house.

Teddy hands me the two totes stuffed with hotel towels and Florida beach hats, while he lugs the suitcases in behind him. We are just inside the door when we hear Perk shout in the kitchen.

"What in the Sam Hill?" Teddy and I drop our bags and run in the house just when she starts reading the note.

> Dear Miss Pauline,
> I told my mother what I did like you told me to. She said I had to make it right with your sister. I don't have any money to give her but she can get fifty dollars for this bird. My mother raises them. They are called Lovebirds but tell her to be careful cause they bite. If you go down to Roses you can buy a cage cheap, but the box here is fine for a day or two. P.S. Please tell your sister the basement door is still unlocked.
> Sincerely,
> Sammy Engels

"Pauline," Perk's shaking her head furiously and backing away from a New Balance shoe box on the kitchen table, the lid covered with holes for air. I can hear the faintest little peeping inside the box, but even I am too nervous to open it. Teddy finally lifts the lid just enough to see the little blue and green bird staring up at him.

"Would you look at this! Is he not the cutest fellow?" Teddy has always been more easy going than Perk and I put together, and even though Perk calls the shots in their marriage, he seems perfectly content to let her. As long as he can buy big screen televisions and invite his bank friends over to watch football, Teddy lives life happy as a clam. Teddy lifts up the lid all the way and sticks his hand in to give the bird a pet, and right when he does the bird stretches out his beak, bites Teddy's hand, then flies straight up and out of that box and up onto the kitchen ceiling fan blade, which is thankfully not on. He is looking down at the three of us through his little bird eyes, and I swear he looks like he is plotting an attack. Teddy runs into the bathroom to get something for his bite, and Perk runs in after him. I am left standing there, watching.

The bird stares back. I don't know why but it occurs to me that I haven't washed my hair this week. There isn't that much of it since I cut it short a few years back, but that bird might think it's plenty for a nest. I start backing away slowly, until I feel the bathroom door against my shoulders.

"Perk," I say, "let me in."

"No," she says. "I am not letting you in here while that bird is loose."

"Perk, I mean it. Let me in. That bird is flying in your living room right now. Quick, now."

I can hear Teddy behind the door telling her to let me in. The door opens a crack and I slide myself in before Perk slams it shut again.

"This," she says, "takes all."

"It all happened Saturday," I explain, practically spilling over the words to get them all out, "when you were supposed to get home. I came over to check on things and found this boy coming out of your basement."

"How," Perk says, "did a boy get in our basement?"

Teddy is looking down real hard at his shoes. He shrugs his shoulders a few times like he is holding a discussion with his shoes, then finally looks up at Perk.

"Teddy," Perk says, "I told you to lock that door. Oh, good lord, what did he take, Pauline?"

"Oh, he was just a baby, Perk, not even fifteen. His friends dared him to prove he was tough, that's all. He didn't take a thing but that old garlic press you left in the basement." At that Teddy starts chuckling, and before long he is doubled over laughing. "See Perk," he says, "Rosetta told you a stranger would be coming into your life. Looks like he came while we were away. Or maybe she meant the bird!" Perk does not look amused. Laughing, Teddy goes on. "When we got to that place, Pauline, that Pizza Hut/Psychic Highway Rest Stop, Perk didn't even want to go in. She was going to stay in that taxi but I dragged her out. Rosetta had already walked over to the door and said, "This is your future calling, Perk, do not be late."

"I wanted to just smack her, Pauline," Perk says, shaking her head.

"So we go through the door and Madam Sherie, that's who greets us, she takes one look at Perk and me and Rosetta and tells Perk she can stay. Tells me my aura is off. I had to go to the waiting room which was just a booth at the front of the Pizza Hut. And Madam Sherie gives Rosetta a hug and then Rosetta turns around and says she's going outside for a smoke." Teddy stops to take a breath and starts laughing again.

"Madam Sherie takes Perk over to the kitchen but all the equipment is gone so it's not really a kitchen and there's a red curtain across it and she draws it so I can't see in. I am just sitting there, Pauline, wondering what in the world an aura is, and I hear Perk saying, "NO, just NO" from behind the curtain. I can't exactly hear what Madam Sherie is saying but Perk, there is no mistaking, is not having it, whatever it is. I'm about to walk back there when I see out the window a green Ford Escort pull up, and Rosetta climbs in the front seat. And leaves. Just like that, without even saying goodbye."

"That woman," Perk adds, "ought to be in prison."

"And then Perk comes back looking about as mad as I have ever seen her and tells me to pay the woman. I had to pay Madam Sherie one hundred dollars for five minutes of nothing, according to Perk, and I don't mind saying that was more than we spent eating out for six whole days."

Teddy is leaning back against the sink, and Perk's sitting on the toilet with the lid down, and I'm looking at both of them and I just have more questions than I can get out. And before I choose one, we hear chirping, chirping on the other side of the door.

"Perk," I say, "what do you want me to do? Call animal control?"

"No," Perk says." I don't want to wait that long. Those droppings are going to be all over my oriental rugs and there is just no telling what kind of bugs that thing has brought with it."

Perk walks right out the door. Down on the floor, looking up at her, the bird looks about as harmless as can be. Perk has never been an animal person. For a second I'm afraid she's going to lean over and smack it, but instead she says to that bird, "You, come with me," and bends down and holds out a finger and that bird hops right up on her finger. Just like that. And then Perk walks back into the kitchen and puts that bird back in the box. But she leaves the lid off. I could have been watching Wild Kingdom, it was that surprising.

"Teddy," she says, "go over to Roses and buy a cage and whatever birds eat. And Pauline, don't you dare tell Mama or anyone else about what happened to us in Florida. It's not our finest moment."

"I think it's funny," I say. "And besides, you had yourself an adventure."

"Of sorts," she says under her breath.

"We've all been there ... remember Reggie? But Perk, why in the world would you get excited over a silly psychic? I can see Teddy falling for that, but you?"

"Pauline, between caring for Mama and worrying about James, I needed to cut loose and forget myself for a minute." Perk is fidgeting, moving around dish towels that have no business but to be right by the sink, looking at me and shaking her head. The bird has begun chirping.

"What in the world is going on? You don't even like animals," I say, looking over at the bird.

Perk sits down at the kitchen table, glances over at the box where the bird sits chirping, staring up at her. "That awful woman told me Teddy was going to leave me, that he was going to take off down a psychic highway that didn't include me. I know it's a load of nothing, Pauline. I know that for a fact. But when you opened the bathroom door just now, and I saw this little thing staring up at me, I thought to myself, well, we could use a little company." Perk looks up at me, shrugs her shoulders. I miss James. I know he's busy with his work, but I miss his face. Teddy does too, but you know Teddy, he won't tell him. Every Saturday when he calls I say, "Come home,

James. Tell Darlene we can all drive down to Williamsburg to shop the outlets. He works too hard, but he won't listen." Perk sighs and looks down at the bird, staring up at her. "I haven't said this to Teddy, but I am worried James and Darlene are having problems. Marital problems."

Perk and I sit at her kitchen table, waiting for Teddy to get back from Roses. An hour has passed and neither one of us has moved from our chairs. The bird has flown straight up out of the box and is now sitting on Perk's shoulder, and every time Perk starts talking he bobs his head up and down, like he is telling the story too. Perk takes no notice whatsoever, but I am having a hard time concentrating on what she's saying.

"Of course I didn't say a thing to Teddy," Perk says. "When that fortune teller told me he was going to be unfaithful, I saw red. I never thought for a minute he would cheat, but it galled me that woman said he would. And you know Teddy, he would have spent the next twenty years proving to me he never cheated, justifying every wink he's ever given a female. So I just told him a fib, said Madam Sherie told me I was going to meet a stranger and that he was going to change my world. And Teddy thought that was the funniest thing he'd ever heard."

At that Perk starts laughing and the bird starts bobbing his head so fast I am convinced it's going to have a stroke. We hear the front door open and Teddy comes in with the birdcage and a five-pound bag of birdseed. Perk stands up so fast the bird ruffles every one of his feathers but still just stands there watching Perk as she starts setting up the cage and opening the bag of birdseed. There's no going back now. Perk's already made the bird a part of the family.

"What are you gonna call it?" I ask.

"Bird. His name is Bird." Perk says.

Teddy and I look at each other and then down at the floor. Once Perk decides on something, there is no discussion.

Bird is touring his new cage that Perk's set on the table in the family room by the window. The cage is shaped out of white wire and looks like a tiny barn, with a little square door and a pencil looking piece of wood across the length for the bird to roost. Perk is already pulling out her fine china teacup and filling it with water when my phone rings. It's Mama.

"My TV is broken," she says before I can even say hello. "That TV you and Perk brought me is broken."

"What's it doing?" I ask.

"I can't watch Jeopardy. The channel changes every minute to something else. It's the sorriest excuse for a TV I have ever seen and I need you to take it back and bring me my old TV."

"I'll be over in a minute."

I start telling Teddy what Mama said and look over and see Perk with her face practically in the cage. Cooing at the bird like he's a newborn baby boy.

Mama's in the bedroom when I arrive, and her first words as soon as I walk through the door are, "What took you so long?"

"Hey Mama." I take a peek around the living room to make sure nothing surprising has happened since I was here last, which was yesterday, but everything is in its place; this year's calendar with all our family pictures sitting on her marble coffee table, her upholstered straight back chair with two pillows and one rubber cushion stacked up on the chair seat. We just kept adding pillows as it became harder for her to get up from a seated position. Any one of us could practically lean against that chair now and be seated. From that chair, you see her paintings, all of them painted by her friend, Mr. Richardson. The portraits of Perk and me when we were in our twenties look like other people to me now,

but Mama loves to stare at them. Almost more than the painting of Majorca, with its windmills and tiny village huts dotting the seaside. She can't remember now why she loves that painting so much, so we all remind her that that was her favorite trip after Perk and I moved to Richmond and she and Aunt Eleanor went traveling. Back when Mama could remember, her eyes would light up like a match got struck, and she'd smile the whole time she talked about Majorca.

In the bedroom I find Mama sitting on the side of her bed. We took off the box spring months ago when she started having trouble getting in and out of bed. Perk went over to her apartment one day and saw that she had put a skinny step ladder by the side of the bed. When Perk asked her where she got it, Mama said she borrowed it from the maintenance man. Not one of us could have used that skinny ladder to climb on without a mishap. Teddy and Perk hauled off the box spring the next day and returned the step ladder to Jeremy. Now Mama barely has to lean in to sit down on her bed.

The TV is blasting from the maple table opposite the bed, sounding like one loud interruption as the channels change every two seconds. It doesn't take me long to figure it out. Somehow Mama has hit the scan button on the remote. The TV is set to show a channel and then after a few seconds or so, scan on to the next channel, and the next, and on and on, till it finally gets back to Jeopardy and Mama gets mad all over again once it disappears to the home shopping network.

"I told you this thing was broken, Pauline. And I'm going to tell you what, you and Perk need to take me to buy a car and you need to go bring my old TV back. I need my car." With that Mama sets her jaw and turns to me with a look that just dares anybody to tell her different.

I don't answer, just walk over and take the remote and start hunting down the duct tape. I know more about television remotes now than I will ever need to know. I get the remote buttons taped up and show Mama the power on and off, volume up and down, and channel up and down, the only buttons not taped up. She's still talking about the car, so I just change the subject.

"Well Mama, you will not believe, but you are a grandmother again, and this time to a bird."

"A what?" she says.

I start laughing, relieved to have the conversation change. "Your daughter Perk has gone and adopted a bird and the thing is eating off her best china."

Mama looks over at me and starts smiling. "Perk doesn't have a lick of sense, but you know Auntie had a bird, when she lived over on Hillside."

Sometimes Mama just plucks a memory out of midair, and it's something so small but exactly accurate. Her mother's sister, Eleanor, who we all called Auntie, who Aunt Eleanor was named after, moved to Roanoke once she was widowed at the age of seventy-one and bought a house not far from Granny, and she brought this little yellow bird with her.

Auntie liked her martinis, and she never did drive a car. Between Mama and Aunt Eleanor, she got driven everywhere. She wasn't but four foot nine and taller than Granny, but they had more fun together than all of us put together. Granny would put a cushion in the Cadillac so she could see over the steering wheel and the two of them would ride the parkway in the afternoons, looking out at the Blue Ridge while Auntie read poetry, holding a thermos of martinis in the other hand with a cigarette burning in the ashtray. She died before Granny did, and we all missed her, but I think Granny missed her most.

"You know, Auntie didn't care all that much for West Virginia and that rich husband of hers." Mama shakes her head.

"I thought she liked being rich," I say.

"Somebody else's wealth always comes with a cost, Pauline. That husband of hers was just plain mean and that coal dust in Morgantown stained every one of Auntie's dresses. She used to say she still felt like she was inhaling coal dust even after she moved back."

Mama's eyes look empty for a second and then they light up and she smiles. "Her husband Bernard built the two of them a mausoleum and put Auntie's birthdate on it, and she made us all swear never to send her back to Morgantown after she died. I suppose folks looking at that mausoleum think she's still living."

We both laugh. "Mama, she was born in 1890, they must think she is the oldest living soul on earth."

Mama smiles again, her eyes filling with a vacancy before twinkling again as she says, "Auntie always said that bird was the best thing that ever happened to her in West Virginia."

I point the taped up remote at the television and change the station to Jeopardy. "There, Mama," I say as I plump up her pillow. "I've got some shopping to do."

Mama has already forgotten about the old TV and the car she needs and waves a hand goodbye as she listens to Alex Trebek announce the next Jeopardy answer on the screen. The volume is so loud I can still hear him talking after I close her apartment door and am halfway down the hallway.

As I'm rounding the corner to the elevator, I spot Jeremy changing a lock on another apartment. He gives me a smile and waves as I walk by. My throat squeezes and I give him the slightest smile. I have never come to terms with what Perk told me about him. That day Perk returned the step ladder to him, he must have been in a chatty mood. She asked him what made him choose this job, and he had laughed and told her his wild days were over. Perk took that as an open invitation to pry, and before you knew it he was telling her he used to be a Chippendale dancer in Baltimore. Perk asked him if he had ever told that to Mama, and he laughed again and said, "Oh yeah, that's how we got to be friends."

According to Jeremy, Mama had told him she and her sister Eleanor went to a Tupperware party one time and the hostess had ordered Chippendale dancers to perform because her husband went out of town and didn't take her. He said when Mama told him that she had laughed and told him never to wait to live it up.

As the elevator stops and I get in, it occurs to me that Mama has always lived it up, in her own way. In spite of loss, she has always managed to find the light behind her eyes and set it shining, as much for me and Perk as for her own self. Most days I can't even remember my eight year old self and the Daddy I once knew, but there has not been a minute in a day when I haven't known that light in Mama's eyes, shining through me even when I could barely see right in front of me.

I used to think I was all alone because I had lost Daddy so young. That the best part of me that lived had died right along with him. It took me losing Carleton to see there wasn't a piece of me that wasn't always a part of Mama, and her a part of me.

Right after Carleton died I had tried my best to crawl under the covers and never come out, but Mama wouldn't have it. The day after he died, she made me dress up and deliver ham rolls to the Johnson house, and listen to Mrs. Johnson sob and grieve her son, all while I sat with my hands folded in my lap, dry eyed and quiet, uncomfortable seeing her cry.

Mama drove me home that day and didn't say a word. Later, when I was curled up in bed, she came in and sat beside me on the bed.

"My life is over," I sobbed. "It's just too hard." The tears pouring out of me had come so fast and hard, all that pain pouring out, I wasn't sure if I was crying for Carleton or Daddy or the both of them. Or me.

She had listened, and then held my face in both her hands and said, "Honey, we all carry our burdens and pain, and we march on." She kissed my forehead then and hugged me close. "The good lord gives us the strength to face our pain, and lifts us when we fall."

Mama smiled then, stroking my hair, and said, "You're just going to have to stick around and tough it out with the rest of us."

6

It's Not Nothing

OF ALL THE TIMES BOB HAS STOPPED by on his mail route there's only been one time when he's talked about himself. I've always thought it was because he was shy but lately, I have come to think it's not that at all. It might not strike someone else as peculiar, but I am starting to think that Bob has got a secret.

Bob is not shaving. That might not seem like much, but he always has a smooth face. Until a month ago. There are only a few reasons Teddy stops shaving, and none of them are good. He might be sick or mad at Perk or holed up in their den for days watching all of the NFL playoff games. Until Perk puts her foot down and then, just like that, the next time I see him his face is as smooth as a newborn baby.

Today, I have decided, I am going to ask Bob about this. I can see by my wall clock it is 4PM and that is close enough to the time when Bob brings the mail. I put on a pot of coffee and pull out the Girl Scout Thin Mints I've been keeping in the freezer since March. Bob and I talked once about our favorites, and even though he said shortbread, he also mentioned Thin Mints were close to the top of his list.

I can hear the storm door opening and the whoosh of mail spilling in through the slot. I can't remember the last time

82

Bob didn't hand my mail to me personally. I walk out to the living room and have just gotten the front door open when I see the backside of the tiniest wisp of a girl in a mail uniform walking down the sidewalk, talking to someone through the ear buds hanging down from each side of her head.

"Hey," I call out. She stops, turns around, and waves to me.

"Where's Bob?" I say. She appears to be no more than nineteen or twenty, and I wonder to myself if she is even old enough to be a responsible mail carrier.

She grins. "He retired." With that she turns around, starts talking through her earbuds, and walks on to the next house. I am undone, to say the least. Bob did not mention he was retiring, and he was just by here yesterday. It's enough to make a body feel robbed of something they didn't even know they had.

I walk back into my house and straight back to the kitchen. I start pacing, back and forth, until I have paced by the kitchen table so many times I finally grab a Thin Mint as I walk by. My thoughts are in a tug of war about what to do next, what to think next, and how in the world to digest the news that Bob is no longer my mailman.

There are times in your life when the big news comes and you know exactly what to do. And then there are those times when news comes and you don't exactly know how it is going to affect you until you hear it, and then it comes and you realize it is big news and you have no idea what to do. This is one of those times.

I'm halfway through the plate of Thin Mints when I hear a knock at the front door. I grab another Thin Mint and pop it on my way to answer it. I am chewing the last little morsel when I open the door and see Bob standing there, grinning from ear to ear. He looks different without his uniform on, but even with a plaid shirt and khaki pants on, he looks just as good. And I don't even brush the crumbs off my face. I just start smiling.

Bob steps into the living room and before he can even start telling me the news, I say, "Bob, you are a surprise. Come on back to the kitchen." I can barely hold in my joy, my relief that Bob is here, not gone, and it is all I can do not to rush over and give him a hug. I don't, but a part of me feels like I already have.

He walks back to the kitchen and as he sits down and slouches back against the straight back cane chair, sprawling his long legs underneath the table, he has the same grin on his face he came to the door with.

I walk over to the coffee pot and pour us both cups, careful not to spill as I set them on the table in front of us.

"Pauline," he says, and he says my name as easy as if he's been saying it all his life. I am immediately struck by his familiar tone, and, truth be told, I like it.

"Pauline," he says, "I wanted to tell you I was retiring a month ago."

Bob is looking at me like he has opened the mystery box and the clues have been revealed. And I don't have the foggiest idea what he is getting at. I have never been one to pretend I know something when I don't. It's not that I am against pretending, I am just not good at it, and I do believe that when you realize a weakness it is always best to own up to it.

So I say, "Bob, you are not making a whole lot of sense." I take the last Thin Mint off the plate without a thought and start chewing. At this point I have lost count how many Thin Mints I have eaten.

"Pauline, I won't miss a thing about delivering mail except knocking on your door and seeing your pretty face smiling at me when you open it, and I thought if it was all right with you I would stop by and visit."

My face heats up so quickly I stand up and turn around. If I were to see a mirror right then I don't think I would recognize the shade of red staring back at me. Bob is busy sipping coffee. I pour myself another cup of coffee and sit down, sipping right along with Bob.

"I'll be honest, Bob. I would miss you if you didn't." I look right at Bob's pretty blue eyes then and give him a wink. Where that boldness came from I do not know, but I sure am glad it came.

It is almost dinner time when Bob leaves my kitchen, and I am not entirely sure he would have left if Perk hadn't called. I could've listened to him going on and on about himself. It was not a bit boring, listening to his stories of growing up in South Hill, his daddy's drinking himself to death and his Mama's cancer when he was in high school. I could feel our bond grow inside me. I came close to telling him about losing Daddy, that's how close to Bob I felt right then. I didn't, but just thinking I could brought a freshness to my smile as I sat there. He was talking more in one hour than he had in the whole six months I'd known him. Bob's eyes lit up when he talked about his Mama, how she would cook him a full breakfast every morning and bake him pies that would make him drool, and tell him he was handsome as he was walking out the door for school. It was like the puzzle pieces of Bob were finally fitting into place.

When Perk calls she must have a sense, because she immediately asks, "What got you in such a good mood?" I look over and see Bob already on his feet and waving to me as he heads for the door.

"Pauline, are you listening?" Perk shouts. "That woman from Mama's called me again. Laura has got to be the biggest flake around. Telling me Mama had to be wheeled back to her apartment because she got too tired on her walk. I mean, Pauline, what are they getting paid for over there?"

"Is she hurt?" I say as I wave to Bob. He is already closing the door but I am too worried about Mama to feel sad that we didn't get a proper good-bye.

"No, but I almost told that flake the money we spend there should include helping out old people when they get tired on their walks. She made it sound like Mama was about to keel over and die."

"Is she alright?" I ask. I am still feeling the warm glow of having Bob near me, at my table, and listen to Perk as if she is in the background.

"She is fine," Perk laughs. "I made Teddy drive over with me and when we got there she was sitting at her kitchen table with a pint of ice cream and a spoon. And when I asked her how she was feeling, she said, *"Fine, When are you going to take me to buy a car*?" You know, Pauline, sometimes Mama's memory is sharper than all of us put together. Out of the blue today she says, 'whatever happened to Pauline's friend, Carleton Johnson?' Teddy and I looked at each other and almost dropped our teeth. How many years has it been since high school, fifty? I don't even know what made her think of him, but she sure knew who she was talking about."

"Pauline," Perk is saying, "do you know when I reminded Mama that Carleton died the day of your graduation, she looked at me and said, *'No mother should ever bury a child.'* And then she sighed and went back to eating her ice cream."

Just hearing Perk say Carleton's name out loud hurts my heart, even after all these years. Mama's timing has always been uncanny, almost like a knowing she has about things that haven't happened yet. The fact that she mentioned Carlton on the same day Bob was here reminds me that

Mama's always had some kind of sixth sense. And knowing that Mama remembers that Carleton was my first love, my only true love, makes my heart hurt a little more. People can talk all they want about moving through their grief. When the time comes, we all fall back into that hurting, no matter how long it's been, how far we've come.

"Pauline," Perk keeps going. "Teddy did the shopping today and bought a pot roast big enough to feed an army. I have it in the oven now and he said to tell you there is a mandatory family dinner tonight and you are required to attend. Six o'clock. I should warn you while he was at Kroger's he came up with some ideas and he won't tell me about it until you get here."

I hang up and look over at the empty plate of cookies and Bob's coffee mug, still halfway full. My heart tugs hard. I am missing Bob, even though he just left a few minutes ago.

I check the clock and see I still have enough time to take the trash out before I go to Perk's house. I keep the super can out in the alley. It's just a short walk from my back door, and I believe that is exercise, no matter how short a walk. The forsythia and rose bushes form a nice line along my back fence, and a low rock wall separates the bushes from the alley. The rock wall came first. Over twenty years ago, Reggie talked me into buying flat James River rocks from a guy he knew, rocks I imagine he either stole from a quarry or private land somewhere on the James. Reggie built that wall for me, told me it was the least he could do for lending him the two-thousand dollars he needed to buy his plumbing tools. I still shake my head sometimes when I walk past it, those rocks stacked loosely, some sticking out, some sticking in. We would sit out back on the lawn chairs and from time to time Reggie would point at that wall, look at me, and say, "I sure did a good job, there, don't you think Pauline?" and every time I would say, "Sure did, Reggie."

After Reggie went to jail, I bought the bushes at Lowes and planted them right in front of that wall, hoping to cover up the sight of it and any mention of Reggie. They are a pretty sight to see now, towering tall over the wall. When Reggie was building it, during the sticky summer evenings after he'd come home from work, he'd pull on an old pair of cut-offs and spend a few hours out there, his radio blasting, singing along to George Strait. I didn't know it then, but he was taking those prescription pain medicines he sold, too. No wonder that wall is as sloppy as he was staggering back to the house, on any evening after he'd been working on that wall. I'd thought he was working so hard back then. I don't know why I never had someone tear that thing down. Maybe we all need reminders of the mistakes we make in life, spotlights on our vulnerable sides, showing us the fool we can be. I can look at it now and almost not even think about Reggie, so much time has passed.

I put the trash bag in the super can and turn to head back inside. The sight of a loose rock, sticking out more than usual, catches my glance and I stoop down to push it back. There is something solid inside, something that is blocking my hand from pushing it back in place. As I pull the rock toward me and stick my hand in the hole, I feel something like paper and I pull out the wad, a green chunk of money that I drop as quick as if it's a hot potato. Bills of money fan out like a deck of cards, twenties and tens and who knows what denominations behind the ones I can see. My breath catches and I turn all the way around to see who is there.

The alley is empty, quiet, and the houses backing up to it are still, my neighbors out of view. There is no reason in the world for me to feel guilty, but as I snatch up the money I

feel dishonest, like I am robbing somebody of what is theirs. I start to panic trying to make a decision, do I leave it where I found it or call the police? We find out who we are when the hard choices appear. Holding the wad of money, I rush back to the house, drop it in my pocketbook and head out the door to Perk's. I'll count it when I get there. Perk will know what to do.

I get to Perk and Teddy's in record time, that money burning a hole in my thoughts the whole ride over. I have already decided I am going to call my third district police station and report it. The cash is tucked deep inside my pocketbook. I take several deep breaths and use my key at the door.

Perk is standing by the stove, the bird perched on her shoulder like a supervisor overseeing the job at hand. I can hear Teddy down in the basement moving something big across the floor, but I don't even stop to look down the stairs.

"Perk," I say.

I hold up my pocketbook so fast the bird gets spooked and puffs up his feathers and flies off Perk's shoulder and up onto the ceiling fan blade before I can even say "Look." Opening up my pocketbook, I pull out the wad of cash. "I found this. I don't even know how much is here, but someone stuffed it inside my rock wall back at the alley. I saw a rock loose when I went to take out the trash tonight."

Perk's eyes get wide and she turns from basting the roast and stares at me, her mouth shaping into the largest O I have ever seen. "That must be over $1000," she says.

The only time she's come close to looking like this before was when we drove to an estate sale along the James River. Perk had been excited for days before because she had read that Debbie Reynolds had lived there for a time. The home was just an old tired looking Victorian. When we walked in, both Perk and I could feel this different kind of bad air. It was the coldest darkest kind of place, with the rooms painted dark purple and the furniture upholstered burgundy.

Perk whispered to me, "I am going to have heart failure if I do not get out of this place." We had turned around and left that house right then. Some things you know right away to keep a distance from. When we got back to Richmond, Perk told Teddy about the house. He immediately went to his computer and searched. It turned out Debbie Reynolds had not lived there, she had lived further down the valley. The man who had owned this house in the twenties had been a doctor at the Catawba Hospital, treating tuberculosis patients, and had been arrested for trying out experimental drugs on the help in that house. The article Teddy read said a cook was found choking on her vomit in the living room and ended up dead. His wife had turned him in.

"That," Perk says now, looking at the wad of money, "is trouble, nothing but pot stirring trouble."

Perk and I don't always agree, but this is one time we did. "And," she says, "don't even mention it to Teddy. You know he'll only devise some far-fetched investment for you to spend it on." She turns and goes back to basting the roast.

We had both listened to Teddy's retirement plans for the three of us, the Boston Whaler we would all buy together, the one we would dock in downtown Richmond and serve coffee and donuts to the boaters sightseeing down the James. Even though Teddy knows full well Perk gets carsick just sitting in the backseat of a car. Then there was the limousine service, the one that would require the three of us purchasing a limousine and taking turns driving all times of the day and night. The only thing we all ended up doing was working long enough to retire without worrying about what to do next.

I stuff the money back in my pocketbook and use my cell phone to call the third precinct police station, with Perk listening in. "Officer," I tell the nice young woman who answers the phone, "I need to report some found money. My name is Pauline Smith."

Perk is looking at me and rolling her eyes and motioning with her hands for me to speed it up.

"I'm sorry officer, what? Well, it's a lot. Over a thousand dollars, I think. I've been too busy to count it. I found it stuffed inside my rock wall out by my alley and can only say the stack is thick and there are at least several tens and twenties. What? I would have no idea where the money came from. If I did, I would not be calling you. Donate it? Thank you very much." At that, I hit the disconnect button on my phone.

Perk is looking at me like I have done something very wrong. When, in fact, I have done nothing but try to be a good citizen. And the police told me to keep it. Unclaimed money on personal property is considered the property owner's money. And just like that, I am rich, or at least richer than I was two hours ago. Except this does not feel good, it feels wrong.

"I want nothing to do with this, Perk. It's going right back where I found out it, beside that sorry wall, just as soon as I get home."

"Sounds right enough," she says.

The bird hasn't stopped chirping since I arrived, until now. There is a quiet that fills the kitchen and without saying a word Perk turns from the stove and walks away. I can hear her cooing as she climbs the stairs. Moments later she is back at the stove, stirring the pot roast, Bird settled and quiet on her shoulder.

We are setting the table and deciding what groceries to take Mama for the week when Perk's phone rings.

"Grand Central," she says, shaking her head, before answering with a long drawn out "Hellooooooooooooooo."
Bird takes that as his exit and lifts off her shoulder, landing on the ceiling fan blade, still turned off. I don't think Perk has let Teddy turn the fan on ever since Bird arrived.

I am putting down forks and knives and glance over at her. Perk is standing by the stove, staring at the cooked pot roast, listening to someone with a lot to say, apparently. There has always been a tell with Perk, a tiny shift in her hips and straightened back that shows you she has switched from casual to serious.

"I see," she says, "No, I have medical and durable power of attorney and no one is taking my mother anywhere until I get over there. We are on our way. Thank you."

Of all the times I have heard my sister on phone calls with salesclerks and security guards and strangers standing in line at the movie theatres, I have never once heard her say less. Now she turns and looks at me with that same wide-eyed stare and mouth turned up in an O shape that means trouble.

"Jeremy found Mama on the stairs, between the third and fourth floors. She told him she was resting, and he called down for a wheelchair."

"Did she fall?" I ask.

"They don't know. She's back over at the apartment but that personalized living supervisor Laura wants to send her to the hospital." Perk rolls her eyes.

"Come on Pauline. Teddy," she shouts as she's turning off the stove burner and carrying the pot roast to the refrigerator. "We've got to go to Mama's. Now."

I sit in the front with Perk as we ride over. Teddy's in the back fooling with his smartphone, and Perk is driving like she is on a racetrack. There is not much that unsettles Perk, but when anyone starts telling her what to do about Mama, she gets ruffled. Ruffled with a steeled purpose. This woman has ruffled her, and I can see Perk mapping out every possible retort to anything that woman is going to bring at her.

"Those people have no experience dealing with a healthy 96-year-old woman," she says. "Who wouldn't get tired climbing those steps?"

"The elevator in that building is never working," I say, thinking about all the times I've had to wait for the only working elevator to show up.

Perk looks over at me and nods. Laura has called us both before, asking us to stop Mama from using the fire stairs. We both have told her more than once that Mama grew up believing you climb stairs to stay healthy, and if there is one soul who wants to stay healthy, it's Mama.

Jeremy told Perk one time that people at Serenity call Mama "the walker". They see her all times of the day walking down the halls and breezeways, smiling at everyone like she knows them when in fact she wouldn't remember any of them from one walk to the next. And using her whole little body to open the fire door before walking down a flight and across a building and then back up a flight on her daily route. We all know the route.

I look over at Perk and I can see her formulating. She keeps her eyes fixed on the highway and says, "You know, this does feel different. I would never say it to that woman, Pauline, but we might need to make some changes."

I nod, knowing that even though I hadn't had the same thought, it is the right one.

7

Clear Headed

WE ARRIVE AT MAMA'S APARTMENT BUILDING just as an ambulance is leaving. The lights are not flashing, a good sign that Mama isn't on her way to the hospital. We are parked and inside waiting on the elevator within ten minutes. I don't even have to look over at Perk to know she is steeled and ready for a fight. Teddy has not said two words since coming up from the basement, and seems hypnotized by whatever he is watching on his smartphone.

The doors open and Jeremy walks out, smiling when he sees us. I am five shades of red as I have still not been able to shake that image of him as a Chippendale dancer or stop feeling a guilty attraction whenever I see him. The chance meeting in the grocery store stirred something inside me, a thrill that scared me, a feeling I just didn't have any room for. I avert my eyes and look down.

"Hey, ladies. Teddy. Your mother is okay. She's with an aide and Laura," he says.

I can feel Perk tightening the grip on her pocketbook.

"Thank you so much for helping her," Perk says, looking at him with a firmness that doesn't match her light tone of voice. "I have always said if Mama ever needed any help, she is in the right place to find it."

"No telling how long she was sitting there," Jeremy says, crinkling his brow, the worry lining his face. I want to reach over and console him, tell him how strong our Mama is, but I know he's already crossed the line with Perk. He is just not savvy enough to see that she is baiting him.

Perk looks at him and smiles. "Well," she says, "Mama is a patient woman."

Jeremy steps out of our way as we take over the elevator, and Perk maintains eye contact and smiles at him until the doors close.

"These people," she complains as we go up to the eighth floor, "you would think they would expect these things to happen and deal with them, instead of throwing up an alarm every time an old person falls down."

I use my key to enter Mama's apartment and the three of us step through the doorway and into the living room. Mama is seated on her chair with the three cushions stacked in the seat, sipping on a bottle of Welch's grape juice. The aide is seated beside her, and Laura is standing over, apparently giving Mama a quiz in a very loud voice.

"Mrs. Smith, can you tell us what day it is?" Laura leans down, her thin framed glasses halfway down her nose, speaking in clipped sentences like she is giving marching orders. Her face is loose with wrinkles and her bottle-blonde hair sticks up in spikes from her head, and I cannot decide if someone took a chunk off by mistake or if she is going for a look and hasn't quite succeeded. Laura wears a badge clipped to a chain around her neck and taps it every so often like a twitch she can't control. It reads 'Serenity Senior Solutions Supervisor'.

We hear Mama respond before she even looks our way. "Not until I see today's paper," she tells Laura, "and it didn't come today."

Mama looks our way and says to no one in particular, "Who called them?" then smiles in that way where you see her whole face lit up.

Laura straightens up when she sees Perk, like she knows the fight that is coming. In a voice that is just filled with reproach, Laura says, "Could we speak outside?"

Perk smiles and says in a voice loud enough for the hallway to hear, "anything you want to say to us, Laura, you can say to Mama."

There is a line in the sand that has been drawn between Perk and Laura, and the rest of us are waiting on the sidelines. My sister has always been composed under pressure, with a will sharp enough to cut a bone. When Perk and I were kids, Mama's parents lived across the alley from us. After Daddy died, Mama would walk across the alley every day around 4pm and have a glass of sherry with Granny in the sunroom. Grandaddy was usually at the hospital, but on the off times when he was home, he would be out there, smoking a cigar and sipping a sherry along with them. Most days Perk would tag along too, and lay up on the chaise longue with a ginger ale and sip along like she was one of the adults, listening to every word they said. She heard Mama telling Granny about single men trying to court her, how the eligible bachelors were all either alcoholics or had less money than she did, and Granny telling Mama not to suffer fools. And when Grandaddy would sit out there getting all worked up because the HCA was trying to buy the hospital, he would practically sizzle with anger, talking about the HCA kicking out the hard-working doctors and nurses who had spent a lifetime saving folks.

Perk was sprawled out on the chaise longue listening to Grandaddy rant about standing his ground against the hospital one afternoon when he had his stroke. Mid-sentence,

Grandaddy's back went stiff and his hand tightened up and bent like a broken arrow. All the commotion that followed, and the ambulance and the rush to find me out in the neighborhood and get me home while Mama and Granny went to the hospital, must have called up in Perk that steel reserve she can draw on now when she needs it. Or maybe she was born with it. I suppose it was there all along, just waiting for a chance to show itself. After that, Perk distrusted hospital corporations. I think she always put the blame for Grandaddy's stroke on what was going on with the HCA buyout. Granny and Mama and Aunt Eleanor spent the next month driving back and forth to that hospital, while Grandaddy lay in a bed with half his body paralyzed and his eyes popping wide whenever anyone of us came to visit. He couldn't speak a word, and that was the saddest thing. Grandaddy loved to talk.

Meanwhile, Aunt Eleanor was still in mourning. Her husband Uncle Brad had died six months earlier of pancreatic cancer, died within a month of finding out he had it. We had all gone to the funeral, and even though I had been going to church all those years since Daddy died, sitting there, staring at his coffin, I couldn't hold back my tears. And I hadn't even liked Uncle Brad.

The day Grandaddy was buried I refused to go to the funeral. I told Mama I wasn't going, and she looked about as sad as I'd seen her. "Pauline, I want you to come with us. Granny wants you to come with us. But this is your choice to make." She sighed and started pulling up her stockings, calling out to Perk to hurry up and get dressed.

I sat up in my room, watching Granny and Grandaddy's house, watching Granny and Mama and Perk and Aunt Eleanor and the cousins pack into two cars and leave for the church. Hester was down in our kitchen, cooking a chicken. "Pauline, come down here," she called up to me.

I waited until the cars had driven off, then walked down to the kitchen.

"Stir the beans while I turn this chicken, please." Hester didn't even look over at me, just stood bent over the stove.

As soon as I found a big spoon and started stirring, she said, "Why didn't you go to your Grandaddy's funeral?"

"I have had enough death, Hester. And funerals."

"Pauline, you are twelve years old and there is as much death ahead of you as there is joy. Don't miss any of it."

That day I had stomped back upstairs not thinking a minute about what Hester had said. It would be years later before I began to see what she had meant. Life follows death no matter how hard you grieve. Celebrating life is as important as doing the grieving.

"Your mother," Laura says now, "has been very happy here at Serenity, but as we all know, the time comes when we all need more help. In the two years she has been here, her falls have become more frequent and her need for assistance has grown. We have assisted living right next door, and I think moving her there would be a benefit to your mother. It would be a shame for something to happen. I'm surprised you would let her live alone." Laura looks over at Mama and sighs. "This is really in her best interest." Laura raises her eyebrows for emphasis and smiles through her teeth, like she is clamping down on a stick to hold back a pain.

I don't dare look over at Perk, and Teddy is busy showing Mama the latest pictures on his smartphone of James and his wife vacationing in the Bahamas. I am a little surprised that Perk hasn't interrupted her, but then I see it.

That timing Perk has when the big things need saying. She is waiting, allowing Laura to grow her confidence. I almost want to warn Laura, but know this is already in the air and Perk has but to take a few more breaths before letting it all out. Laura is already talking about the support care over at the assisted living building when Perk interrupts her.

"Laura, we appreciate everything you are doing for Mama and I want you to know that if we ever do decide to move Mama, we will be looking all over this city, not just here."

Laura's eyes widen into a look like a child has when you have taken their favorite toy away. "We," Perk says smoothly as she smiles, "are working with our Mama on what she wants and what she is capable of doing."

Perk looks over at Mama, sitting atop her stacked cushions, a rim of purple grape juice above her upper lip, smiling. Mama has always had the equal ability of schooling a man or a woman, and it doesn't matter how much of a bully they might be, Mama always speaks her mind directly and with no padding. Perk comes by that naturally. And she stands, no matter the odds.

"Mama," Perk says, "do you want to move?"

Mama's eyes twinkle as she laughs, "Why in the world would I want to move?"

Laura has gone from chatty to dead-eyed silent as Perk goes on. "Mama can heat up her food in the microwave, she walks more than any resident in this entire complex, and my sister and I check on her every day and do all her grocery shopping. If you expect a 96-year-old woman to do more, I'd like to hear about it.

"And," Perk adds, "because I have medical power of attorney, I expect a phone call if you are thinking about sending Mama to the hospital. A little help getting back to her apartment when she wore out was all she needed tonight, and from the sounds of it if I hadn't put my foot down she would already be in the emergency room."

Laura purses her lips likes she's bit into a lemon and stands to go. The aide is still sitting beside Mama, but Perk tells her she is fine to leave too. Mama looks over at them both, smiling.

"Thanks for stopping in," she says.

While Perk is walking them to the door and Teddy is fooling with his smartphone, I help Mama stand up and walk with her back to her bedroom to get ready for bed. She is in her nightgown, laying on the bed, flipping channels until she finds a Law and Order episode, as if none of this has happened. She has already forgotten the commotion she caused. I know the next words out of my mouth are going to fall empty beside her, but I say them anyway.

"Mama, you have got to stop using that fire door walking up all those stairs. They don't like it and it wears you out."

She smiles and her eyes light up again. "Well," she says, "I don't care if they like it or not."

Teddy and Perk come into the bedroom then and kiss her good night. I do the same, and as we are leaving Perk and I decide on a schedule of checking on Mama for the next week or so. "Mama seems to be slowing down," Perk says as we close the door.

"Maybe we need to hire some extra help," I say. "We could do that, Perk."

Perk looks at me like I am speaking another language, but then nods. "Yes, let's do that. I'll call the senior solutions number tomorrow. What do you think, another afternoon visit and maybe one in the evening?"

I am so surprised that Perk has agreed with me I immediately worry that Mama must be worse off than I thought. "Yes, that sounds right," I say.

By the time the elevator opens Teddy is already telling us about a new business venture he has read about for retirees, one involving a dedicated phone line and a police background check. Perk and I listen, ready with the automatic "No" when he asks if we are interested. As we step into the elevator, we see Mrs. Wolf already there. Her back is practically horizontal, she is stooped over so far, and her thick, white hair sticks out like a spotlight on a street corner. She lives across the hall from Mama.

"Why hello, Mrs. Wolf," I say.

She looks over at the three of us. "Do I know you? I am very clear headed but I have a little dementia," she says, looking from one of us to the other.

Perk and I both looked at each other at the same moment. "Mrs. Wolf," Perk says, "where are you going?"

"Home," she says.

Perk reaches over and pushes the open button and helps Mrs. Wolf out the door. Calling back to Teddy and me, she tells us she'll meet us at the car. We can hear her walking down the hall with Mrs. Wolf, talking about NCIS and how much better it was before Tony left the show as the doors close and Teddy and I go down to the lobby.

The three of us drive back to Perk and Teddy's house mostly quiet. The fight's talked itself out of Perk and I'm wrung out from watching it all unfold. I'm turning over in my mind the thought that we are losing Mama, no matter how slowly that is coming. Back at Perk and Teddy's house, we say our good-byes and I drive off with Perk calling after me to come back for pot roast before it turns.

"Those potatoes won't freeze," she says as I pull away from the driveway.

The sight of my own house as I park the car sends a shudder of relief through me that I hadn't known I needed.

I've just turned the key in the front door when my phone rings.

"Hello?" I say. Silence on the other end of the line, so I say it again, "Hello?"

These wrong number calls have me short on patience and I hang up almost right away. This night has not been routine, and I am as frayed as a last nerve plucked clean. I glance down at my loafers, sitting in a neat line by the door, and sigh. They haven't moved in days. I have hardly admitted it to myself but I have to say, I miss that feeling, that wash of love, like something important is happening to me, just me, even if I don't have one clue what it is. I don't need to know, it just is. I've thought of looking under the bed even when I know they are back out by the front door, but don't. You just can't force magic or belief or anything spiritual. It comes natural as a gentle rain.

When we were kids, Perk always read the Nancy Drew mysteries where Nancy solved all the clues and still managed never to get her white gloves dirty. She spent her summers reading in the little room off Granny and Grandaddy's garage and locked the door so I couldn't come in. I would have to beat on the door and then go find Granny before she would let me in. The room had been added as a maid's quarters where the cook, Viney, could come to change into her uniform. It had a chaise longue and a lamp set by the one window and a fan plugged into the only other outlet. There was a bathroom off the room and a door for privacy. All Granny had to do was walk up to the locked door and call Perk's name and as quick as that, Perk would open the door.

I liked the Trixie Belden Mysteries better than Nancy Drew. Trixie was a tomboy and solved clues in her dungarees and flannel shirts. I had a little notebook, just like Trixie Belden, and jotted down everything I saw: what time the mailman came to our house, when Mrs. Lemon walked her Frenchie, how long the milk man let me ride in the back of the delivery truck on Thursdays. Information didn't become a clue until you knew what you were looking at. Follow the clues, Trixie always said.

I am thinking about clues now when my phone rings again. Just as I pick it up, the ringing stops. I am a woman living alone and peace and quiet are part of the life I lead, and my patience has reached its limit. Finding that money, the emergency-that-wasn't-an-emergency with Mama, and now these phone calls. It is more than I have built up a tolerance for. I have always been a woman to look at what can be done, and then do it. Mama taught me that. Clarity of purpose is a comfort to me.

I grab my pocketbook, pull out the wad of money, and march out to the alley. Without even looking around, I throw down the wad of money I am holding and march back into the house, my shoulders a little lighter from the effort.

There is routine that is just getting through the day, and then there is routine that you look forward to. I have always enjoyed the nights when I head back to the bedroom and the TV and a soft nightgown, and a warm bed, thanks to the Target mattress pad. I'm back in my bedroom and turning up the mattress pad to high when I hear it. I have not undressed yet, thank goodness, but the knock on the door is alarming. I am not a woman who normally curses, but I let out a "What in the hell" as I walk to the door.

I have a peep hole in my front door. It came with the house, otherwise I never would have put in the silly thing, but tonight I am relieved it is there. I have to get up on tiptoes to see out of it, and there, standing like a deer in headlights, is Jeb, the high school senior down the street who mows my grass and rakes my leaves and shovels snow off my walks.

Before he was old enough to push the mower, for years Jeb would stop by the house to sell me candy bars for his Boy Scout troop and collect money for church fundraisers. I still can't believe that boy is almost old enough to leave for college.

I open the door and before the boy can speak say, "Jeb, what are you doing here this time of night?"

It is not even 9pm in the summer, but still too late for unexpected visits. Is something wrong at home, has Jeb come to ask me for help? I use my stern voice when I say this, but seeing the worry on his face, quickly add, "Are you alright?"

Jeb is lanky and over six feet, with a long serious face and worry on his forehead he has no business showing at such a young age. His Daddy is an Evangelical preacher in town, and I know, even though Jeb doesn't say it, that his Daddy comes down hard on Jeb. I imagine Jeb is more straitlaced and God fearing than his whole family put together. The boy carries a weight.

"Miss Smith," he says. "I was just walking home by the alley and I found this right beside your wall."

Jeb juts his arm forward and there, just like a bad penny, that same wad of money is clutched in his long teen aged hand, balled up and waiting to be handed back to me.

The boy is holding that money like it's a ball of fire, ready to pass it over to me and be on his way. Of all the people walking down my alley, it had to be Jeb, probably the only honest soul willing to track down the owner instead of taking the money for himself.

My jaw is dropping and I have not one word to say, so instead smile and hold out my hand. There is a resignation that comes with being beat, with seeing the futility of resistance. It is what Mama always says, "sometimes you have to look the other way in order to see where you are going."

"Good night, Miss Smith," Jeb says as he backs away from the door.

The spring in the boy's step is all I need to tell me I made the right decision. I close the front door behind him and drop the wad of money on my hallway table. I will have to figure out what to do with it tomorrow.

8

Florence is a Family Name

A FEW MINUTES LATER I AM SETTLED BACK IN BED and have just turned on the TV when a special bulletin alert scrolls across the screen. The weatherman is saying something about squall lines and river flood stages and power outages, assuring us that they are in close contact with the National Weather Bureau and that they will be our number one source for information throughout this storm. There is something about this weatherman, a smile in his eyes that doesn't go away even when he is reporting on sad news, that is unsettling.

I fall asleep with the TV still on. Sometime in the early morning hours I wake up to a woman selling Instapots. I turn over and fumble for the remote on my bedside table and turn the TV off. The sudden quiet combined with the earliness of the hour and the warm bed are all I need to drift back off to sleep.

I wake later than usual to the sound of rain pounding against the house and my cell phone ringing beside my bed. I answer on the third ring.

"You will not believe this," Perk says without even saying hello.

I sit up and say, "What now?"

"Laura. The woman," Perk takes a breath here, before going on, "called me at nine last night to tell me Mama had fallen asleep with the TV on and was very hard to rouse. And we had just been there hours before. I asked her why and she told me it was a courtesy bed check. I almost told her we did not need courtesy calls, but she was talking so fast I decided to let her talk. Laura said when Mama didn't answer the door, she got maintenance to open it. I didn't even call you, Pauline. When she finally quit talking, I told her that after the day Mama had, I imagine she was worn out. Pauline, I didn't even wait for her to answer. I thanked her and hung up."

"Do you think Mama is all right, Perk?" I have already started to worry, fretting over what else I can be doing for her.

"Pauline," Perk says, "Mama is fine. I am going to stop by at lunchtime and I promise I'll tell you if you need to do anything. There's plenty of days to worry about Mama, but today's not one of them."

Hearing Perk's words calm me down. Mama always used that same tone of voice, the one that was full of strength and reassurance. Mama could punish you with a look that would make you wish you had never gotten in trouble, but she could also soothe you with a voice that made you believe everything was going to be okay.

When Mama drove home the day that Daddy died and called me in from the afternoon game of kick the can in the Sneads' side yard, she stood at the top of the front steps, holding me with a look that felt more like a hug. She bent down then, saying the words, "Daddy died." Mama has always been a woman of direct words.

The words were not the news, Daddy had been sick for a long time with the cancer, but at eight years old I couldn't understand dead. Without even knowing our worlds were changing, I heard Mama's next words over and over in my head, heard her saying, "we are going to be alright." It's surprising after all these years, but I still hear her saying those words whenever I feel despair. "We are going to be alright."

This day has begun abruptly. I make my way into the kitchen for coffee. Outside, I can hear the rains and the wind competing for attention, sending sheets of water against the house, rattling the windows like an intruder intent on getting inside. The gusts are pulling the pine tree branches from side to side out my front window. I glance over at the hallway table and look at the wad of money, sitting like an unwelcome guest setting up a quick claim, daring anyone to kick it out.

There are occasional days when I wake as carefree as a bird, but most days I wake filled with a pressing need to check on Mama. It hasn't always been that way. When I was first on my own, Mama was in the background, a shoulder to lean on when I needed her and as solid as the mountain she lived on. Then the years turned into decades and she was still there, in the background, ready to catch Perk and me when we stumbled, supporting us from a distance as we lived our lives and she lived hers, always happy to see us when we came home for visits or mending us when we were broken, standing on her doorstep with welcoming arms.

It's a common thing and still surprising to understand how that kind of support stays with you, even when the person giving that support slows down. After we moved Mama to Richmond, we saw all the pauses, when she wasn't quite Mama, more like James when he was small. She would demand a car, or to be driven back to Roanoke, without understanding why she couldn't have either one, just wanting what she wanted. Mama had always been in charge of her life. She made good choices, but nobody told Mama what to do. Now, her mind was slowing faster than her body, even though she was also losing her balance, losing her stamina, and falling more. It's a hard thing to see, a sadder thing to watch. But then Mama still has her lucid moments, and even though those shoulders of hers are hunched and more like a bird wing than a bone, I can tell her a story and she'll pick out the kernel of truth in it I usually can't see.

I decide to go check on Mama and just see what she thinks about this wad of money showing up. Maybe even wonder with her why those loafers haven't moved again. I haven't turned the television back on since getting up, and as I make my way to the car with nothing but my pocketbook, raincoat, and rubber rain boots, all the weatherman's talk about squalls and floods are distant wisps in my mind.

I am halfway to Mama's apartment, driving through puddles already spilling over the curbs, trying to navigate the high water, when I decide I better pull over. The water is too high to drive through in my little Ford Focus. Even though it is near eighty degrees and humid as a wool blanket soaked on your skin, my rain boots feel right as I step out of the car and onto the street. Wherever I am going from here, it'll be on foot. I scold myself for not checking the weather before I left the house and start walking, worrying some about leaving my car stranded, but worrying more about how Mama is. Some days that worry for Mama is too strong to put off. Today is one of those times.

My raincoat is pulling and the hood is blowing back as quick as I am holding it on with one hand and holding my pocketbook with the other, the wind and the downpour competing in one continuous roar as I make my way. For a second I wonder whether or not to walk back to the house or continue on to Mama's. The choice pulls at me like the wind on my raincoat. Back and forth, strong both on the side of getting myself home and safe or the other to get to Mama's and check on her. In the end, that pull to Mama is stronger.

Plodding down that sidewalk, I am grateful Mama and I are close enough in size that I will be able to step out of my soaking clothes the minute I walk through her door. At this point, I don't care if I have to wear Christmas sequins as long as it is dry. And Mama has never been skimpy on high quality clothes. For as long as I can remember, anything she bought was classy and good looking. Her other sister Florence was what Mama called a clothes hound, buying new clothes at the bat of an eye and giving Mama her hand-me-downs. Aunt Florence died young of lung cancer even though she never smoked a day in her life, but before she died she filled up a house with pretty clothes. Between what Mama bought for herself and what Aunt Florence gave her you would have thought Mama was made of money. Turned out she was, but nobody ever knew that but Mama and her investment advisor.

I step onto the crosswalk and can see Mama's building up ahead. The road all four ways is nothing but a gushing stream. I have not seen a car the entire time until this very moment when a white minivan with headlights glaring appears through the rain headed right toward me. I am almost to the median and just have time to step up near a Left Turn Only sign before the van drives by slowly, looking for all the world like it is floating down a river. In the passenger seat, someone is turned and looking right at me. My eyes are so smeared from the rain falling I cannot see who it is and hurry on to the other side. Just as I reach the curb I hear a horn blowing. Looking back, I can barely see through the downpour someone leaning halfway out the minivan window.

A young voice, a boy's voice, is calling out, "Miss. Smith, Miss Smith, are you all right?"

I start shouting "Yes, yes" but the minivan has already made a U-turn and is driving back to me. As it pulls up, I see a woman younger than me at the driver's window, motioning me to get in. The minivan stops right there in the middle of the street and Sammy Engels gets out and runs over to me.

"I saw you, Miss Smith," he says excitedly, the rain pouring over his uncovered head like a faucet turned up high. "Come on."

We both climb into the van, me in the front seat and Sammy in the back. I look at the woman driving and can see the resemblance, she has to be his mother, long and lean like Sammy and she has the same large nose and round green eyes. She is smiling.

"I'm Sandy. You must be the Miss Smith who caught Sammy stealing the garlic press." She looks back at Sammy, frowning, then back at me. "I apologize for my son. Isn't this weather just awful? It looks like there are at least three of us crazy enough to be out in it."

I smile back, as much relieved to be out of the rain as anything. "Well you all are life sends, and I can't thank you enough." We are still parked in the middle of the street, but Sammy's mother does not seem in the least bit hurried.

"Where are you headed?"

"Oh just up to Serenity, my mother lives there."

I look over at Sandy to make sure she understands, and she does. Any woman past forty understands that this means I need to check on my parents. Sandy nods and starts the car.

Sammy leans up between our two bucket seats and asks, "Does your sister like the bird? I'm still paying Mom off for that bird, but I hope she likes it."

The fact that the three of us are sitting in the middle of a street with a hurricane blowing all around us does not seem to be a thing either one of them cares about. Sammy sounds so hopeful I don't even dream of telling him what a nuisance I find that bird to be.

"Oh sure, she likes him fine. She's got him eating off her fine china."

Sandy and I both laugh, and Sammy sits back, and lets out a little sigh. "I told Mom I was sorry, but she said I had to make it right. I'm sure glad your sister likes it."

Sandy rolls her eyes and looks back at Sammy, "That doesn't get you off the hook for breaking into the poor woman's home, Sammy. Or stealing."

"I know, Mom, I know." Sammy looks down at his lap and lets out another sigh.

I can see that boy will be made to pay for his mistake for more time to come, but I do feel sorry for him. There is a little part of Sammy that reminds me of Carleton, the part where trouble is always going to find him and he is always going to have to pay for it. Sammy has a good heart just like Carlton did, and I can hope better for Sammy, and pray for him too.

"What brings you all out today?"

"We were just here checking on Sammy's grandmother, Claudine, "Sandy says. "His father's mother. We're divorced." She looks over at me and nods as if this explains everything, then adds, "She's in Bluebird. 512."

"Oh, Mama is in Bluebird, 815."

Sandy laughs. "Practically neighbors. Claudine likes Serenity. Lord, she's been there for over five years now."

Sandy looks back at Sammy, then turns to me. "Does your mother like it?"

"As much as we can hope," I say, thinking of all the times Mama still asks when she is going back to Roanoke. Mama's home roots run deep inside those Blue Ridge mountains. Home for Mama inside her apartment pulses with Roanoke and memory and the heart in the antiques we brought, her loved things. And she is resigned to staying there, but Mama will never be like Claudine, and that is a sadness I have to carry now.

We both nod, and as we pull into the driveway, I turn back to Sammy and say, "Listen to your Mama, Sammy. Always."

"Yes ma'am," he says.

I wave to them both and smile, then step out and head towards the lobby. When I turn back to give them a final wave, Sandy is making another illegal U-Turn as she drives away.

9

Weather In Place

When I walk into Mama's building, the lobby is full of residents sitting around on the three overstuffed couches positioned on three different sides of the room, discussing all the possibilities for what I am now discerning is a hurricane named Florence headed straight for us. If I hadn't been so soaked to the bone, I might have stopped to listen, but wet clothes are only second to dripping boots for misery. Somewhere along the way the rain found its way down my boots and set up a small lake over my feet, the squishing as irritating as the weather has become.

Perk and I didn't grow up with 24-hour news alerts to tell us when a storm was coming or how hard the wind was going to blow or how many inches of rain we were going to get. In Roanoke, in the early sixties, all we knew was what Mama and Daddy told us, or what the one TV channel we got clear reception on announced during the six o'clock news. If you missed the six o'clock news, you either had to wait until eleven PM or else someone had to call you and tell you about any bad weather coming. Or you stepped outside your door.

Nobody talked much about big rains, and the Roanoke River swelled and spilled over its banks plenty, especially after a spring thaw when snow melt came spilling down from the mountains. Not until Hurricane Camille, and even though her flooding practically washed away Nelson County, did you hear about it much before or after in Roanoke. Not like today, where the local weatherman breaks in on any show to report on bad weather, even weather that might or might not happen. It's enough to make you turn off the television and read a good book.

I can barely see out of my fogged-up glasses to press the number 8 button on the elevator, much less to see the blurry figure standing near me. Taking off my glasses helps, and into my view comes the little woman Teddy calls "tumor lady" because the large, inoperable tumor on the left side of her skull forms an almost perfect beret at the top of her head. Mrs. Ruhr is her name. She is always cheery, and I think this is because she is finally home and has no plans of leaving until the tumor takes her. We rode the elevator together a few months ago and she told me she just wasn't going to keep up the chemo nonsense, said she was stopping her treatments and staying put. Mrs. Ruhr is on the fifth floor and has lived here for the past ten years. She told me once she was 92, but to look at her you wouldn't know it. She's as right as rain except for the tumor.

Mrs. Ruhr and I step into the elevator and I make sure to stand far enough away so as not to get her wet. She smiles and I just smile right back. She is not much of a talker and I am not either, so we always get along fine. The elevator opens to her floor, and I wave to her as she walks away, then press the number 8 button again.

Mama's asleep on her bed when I walk in, and I go right to her closet and take out the Kelly green running pants and jacket that were popular forty years ago. I grab a Ralph Lauren polo shirt and head to the bathroom. A hot bath and dry clothes sounds like pure heaven right now. Mama has not stirred and the TV is blasting something about Florence.

Mama must have gotten up when she heard the water running, although I'm not sure how she could hear anything over that TV racket. I hear her at the bathroom door even before I look up.

"Pauline, you are as naked as a jaybird. What are those wet clothes doing on my floor?" Mama's jaw is set and I can see she is irritated, what she would call waking up on the wrong side of the bed. I usually try to change the subject and find a topic that will lift her spirits, but right now I just want a few minutes of peace.

"Mama," I say, rolling my eyes, "I'll get them out of the way as soon as I take a bath. That rain is awful today. Can you give me some privacy, please?" Even though Perk and I grew up with Mama barging into the bathroom when we were taking a bath, to ask a question or answer one we had called out from the tub, today I need some time to soak and relax. That weather has frayed my nerves.

"Well," she snaps, "you are in my house. Go home if you want privacy."

"Mama, please."

"What'd you think was coming with that storm? If your Aunt Florence was alive today she'd be thrilled they named a hurricane after her." Mama turns and walks back to the bedroom.

Even Mama is better informed about Hurricane Florence than I am today. I promise again to clean up after my bath. I am drying my hair with the towel when Mama walks back into the bathroom.

"Did you clean up that mess?"

This is, of course, the first thing I did after climbing out of the tub. Leave it to her to see the one spot I've missed, and it's not until I use the towel I've been drying my hair with to wipe it up that she smiles, and walks back to the bedroom. Mama has always had her way of doing things, and a clean house, an uncluttered house, is what she demands. From all of us. When Perk brought Teddy home from college to meet Mama, we were all sitting in the kitchen, and after he'd put down a cup of coffee and walked out of the kitchen for a minute, Mama had emptied it and washed the cup and put it upside down on the drying rack before he got back. That was the only time Teddy asked where his coffee cup was. He picked up on Mama's ways pretty quick.

I've pulled on the Kelly green running pants and matching jacket when Mama walks back into the bathroom.

"You're wearing that?" she snaps, looking me up and down. I can hear the disgust in Mama's voice, and it digs in and touches on memories of when I was a teen-ager, fighting Mama on every outfit I chose to wear and every outfit she ordered me to wear. I blamed Mama for every insecure feeling and every lonely moment I had back then. It took going off to college and missing her to realize she had been on my side all along.

One time in college I went home for the weekend. Mama had been to the towel outlet in North Carolina and wanted me to pick a set she'd bought me. I sat in front of the television all Saturday and didn't say two words to her. Mama came and went, to work and grocery shopping and finally, in the afternoon, came into the living room and asked me if I wanted to go out to dinner.

"Pauline, you've been sitting in here moping all day long. Let's go out and treat ourselves." Mama eyes lit with a sparkle, a hope.

"No, I don't feel like it." I just rolled my eyes and looked away.

"Now you listen here. You are going to get off your fanny and go get ready for dinner. I don't care if you feel like it or not, we are going out." Mama's eyes had turned to steel and she stood with her arms crossed, her jaw set.

We went out that night, to the Roanoker, and as we sipped on Chardonnay and waited for our flounder plates to arrive, Mama leaned across the table.

"Pauline, you cannot keep blaming me and everyone else for your daddy's death. You are an adult now and you are in charge of how you feel, what you do. Nobody else has that power."

"I know Mama." I had looked down, holding back tears.

"I love you with my whole heart, Pauline, and I am here with you."

"I know that Mama. I just feel so alone all the time. I'm not like Perk. I don't have a Teddy to marry and a home to furnish. It's like I came from another planet."

Mama started laughing then. "Honey, you wouldn't be my daughter if you weren't your own woman. You'll figure that all out, and until then, I know who you are, and I love the woman you are becoming. And I want you to stop looking back and start looking forward. You are a beautiful young woman and the world is waiting for you to know that too."

The tears poured down to my chin, and for once, I didn't mind them coming. Mama and I sat and smiled at each other and ordered a second glass of Chardonnay. In that moment, sitting across from Mama, I knew I would always belong.

I'm fixing us both lunch plates, chicken salad sandwiches on yeast rolls I bought at Kroger's, when the doorbell rings. It's hard to hear anything over the television, but the doorbell rings at a pitch higher than even the television. I answer the door without a thought to how I must look in Mama's dated Kelly green running suit and Christmas socks. It's a new aide.

"Hello, I'm Eloise Smith's daughter, Pauline," I say, puffing out my chest so I come across as an authority while full aware the outfit I am wearing is older than this aide is. "You can skip your visit today since I'm here."

The woman is large, in both poundage and in height, and she glares down at me like I might be a bug she needs to squash. "Humph. She still needs to sign this," she says.

She already has a foot in the door when I nod. "She's in the bedroom." I can't say she would have pushed on past me, but the look of her glaring down at me scared me just a little. I follow her back to Mama's bedroom and don't say a thing more.

Perk and I know from past experience that some of the aides at Serenity steal. We found out the hard way after Perk checked Mama's banking account and saw where she had cashed a three-hundred-dollar check made out to herself in her building's bank branch and didn't have a penny in her wallet the next day. Perk closed the account. We leave ten one-dollar bills in her wallet now and count them every time we visit.

We've had to learn the tricks of leaving Mama in independent living and making sure she isn't being taken advantage of or isn't losing her own way. The day I walked in at lunchtime and saw Mama, seated at the kitchen table, eating her chicken pot pie and sipping on a pony of Sutter Chardonnay like it was her regular coca cola, I saw the lines blurring, Mama mixing up lunchtime for dinnertime, changing a well-worn pattern of sipping a glass of wine with dinner and not before. Perk and I started diluting the wine, bringing her the ponies of Chardonnay with most of the wine poured out and water filled up to the top. Mama remarked more than once that it tasted like water, and when we told her that was because her taste buds were old she had looked at us and said, "Well I can taste lasagna just fine." Finally, Perk told her it was light wine for seniors. Teddy says now Mama is better hydrated than she has ever been, and he is not wrong.

The aide walks out of Mama's bedroom and is on her way out of the apartment without even a thank you when I say, "I hope you have a good day."

She looks back at me and her eyes turn soft. Smiling just the slightest, she says, "I hope you do too."

Even unfriendly people sometimes respond to kindness. Mama taught me that.

Outside the rain is still coming down in sheets. I can look down from the living room bay window and see the parking lot is filling, some cars swamped all the way up to their wheel wells. I picture my Ford Focus parked down the street, filling with water and washing away, and a surge of panic takes hold. There is not a thing I can do now but wait, and that loss of control overwhelms me, my heart beating as fast as a ticking clock. I'm about to call out for Mama to come look at the parking lot, when I turn and see her already in the kitchen, leaning over the counter, eating from the plate I've fixed her. My shoulders drop at the sight of her, relaxed and safe, and I push the thought of my floating car to the back of my mind.

I can't say the wind blowing is an alarming thing, not when Mama and I are eight floors up in a sturdy brick building twelve floors high with no trees close by. I can't feel the slightest bit of sway from the living room where I still stand looking out the bay window at all the rain gushing down in little creek and river lines through the parking lot below us. That time Hurricane Camille blew through Roanoke the panes in all the windows rattled and Mama made the three of us and the dog go down to the basement. We could hear the chestnut tree limbs in Granny's side yard breaking and the rain smacking at the bay window we huddled under. It wasn't long before the winds died down, but the rains kept up for hours.

I can't say I have any thought now but that I am hungry and ready for my chicken salad roll in the kitchen. Mama has already finished her sandwich and stands hovering by the sink eating Haagen Daz Chocolate Decadence ice cream from the pint container with a serving spoon. She holds her cane with the other hand and leans against the counter. I can't tell if her mood has lightened or if she's just busy eating.

I am halfway to the kitchen when I hear Mama's phone ringing in her bedroom. Another wonder, the ring loud and high enough to compete with the television. I answer the phone on the third ring and hear Perk saying, "Mama, what took you so long?"

If I didn't know Mama was right there in the apartment with me, I would swear I was hearing her on the phone. All three of us sound the same, and all three of us sound like Granny, those North Carolina mountain roots run deep in the sounds and the cadence of how we talk. I can tell us apart, but barely. The older we get, the more the words we choose could be coming straight from Mama's mouth. Or Granny's.

"It's me, Perk."

Perk laughs. "What are you doing there? I told you I was going to stop by." She stops laughing for one second and then I hear her yelling, "Teddy, you don't need to go to Pauline's. She's with Mama."

"I thought I'd check on Mama," I say, "and got halfway here and the roads washed out."

Perk is still laughing. "Pauline," she says, "check your phone. We've been calling you for the last hour, worried you were hurt by the tornado."

I can't quite hear the next part of what Perk is saying as she is rushing through a whirlwind of information about trees and roofs coming down in my neighborhood. I look over at the television and see the weather map with the city of Richmond lit up in red with clustered yellow cones dotted all through the neighborhoods near where Mama and I live. Despite seeing the tornado path cones, though, I feel perfectly safe right here. Besides, I cannot imagine Mama sitting in an evacuation center, in a room crowded with other people on uncomfortable chairs and no television. I am surprised the cable hasn't gone out.

"Pauline," Perk says, "even if they try to evacuate Mama, don't let them. Once this clears up, Teddy and I can come get you both."

Sometimes I am amazed at how Perk and I come to the same conclusions independently and with no discussion. Especially when it comes to Mama, but that may be in large part because Mama is an easy book for us both to read. What she needs, what she expects, and mostly what her limits are.

"Are you okay?" I ask.

"Oh, fine," Perk laughs easy as if we were talking about her next vacation, "Teddy already went to the store and stocked up in case the power goes out. You would think we were preparing to be without food and power for months. It would put Granny's fallout shelter to shame."

We both laugh. Granny had a root cellar filled with cans of soup and tins of sardines and Vienna sausages and mason jars filled with canned peaches and gallon jars of water. That dirt floor and the brick walls always smelled damp and musty, and one light bulb hanging down from a string from the wood beam in the ceiling shone a light blinding anyone standing directly in front of it.

Perk and I grew up with drills at elementary school on what to do if a bomb fell or the Communists came. We all knew you got under your school desk first, then waited for the teacher's instruction before filing single file out the door and standing in a circle on the playground until they said you could go back in. Those drills sent a scare through every one of us, and made me certain the fallout shelter in Granny's basement would be our home someday. Over the years the peaches in the root cellar faded from orange to yellow and the light bulb was changed out and a new one screwed in. Mama packed up the sardines and the Vienna sausages after Granny died and took them downtown to the food bank. We ate all the peaches. Mama and Aunt Eleanor sold the house with the root shelter empty and a fresh lightbulb screwed in.

When the new owners moved into Granny's house, Mama took over a pie she'd bought at Kroger's. The wife told her how much they loved the house, and the yards, and even the old dirt cellar. Mama had laughed and told her they used it as a root cellar and a bomb shelter. The woman was so interested Mama kept talking. She told her the story of the time when she was a child, growing up in the house, and a patient had brought Grandaddy a truckload of peaches as payment for a surgery. It was in the thirties and not many people had money. Granny asked her cook, Viney, to mix up a dozen jars of sliced peaches with sugar and cinnamon sticks. She'd decided to make peach brandy, and the recipe called for the jars to be buried deep in the ground for two years to ferment. Granny had Viney go out to the side yard and bury the jars. Nobody saw her bury them. Granny was busy with the baby, Aunt Florence, and Mama and Aunt Eleanor were in school. About a year later, Viney died of a heart attack. Granny had her yard man Leonard out there digging in that side yard for years, looking for those jars. He never did find them.

After I tell Perk about the new aide, she asks me. "Did you check Mama's pocketbook?"

"Of course," I say. "She's got eight dollars left."

"I cannot," Perk says, "believe those people would steal dollar bills. She had ten dollars yesterday. That's it. We are not putting any more back, and when Mama complains, I am going to tell her those aides are stealing her money and if she wants to give her money away she can donate to the Red Cross."

I hang up after promising to call her back once I get home. I have already decided that I am not going anywhere until the rain has stopped. Mama comes back into the bedroom.

"Who were you talking to?" she says.

"Oh, just Perk, she and Teddy said to tell you hi and that they'll see you a little later."

I wipe off the dark mustache line of ice cream from Mama's face with one of the embroidered handkerchiefs she has had for as long as I can remember, a small piece of cloth now as thin a cotton as is possible without falling apart.

"You are ruining it," she says.

"That's what they are there for," I reply.

She walks over to her dresser and begins brushing her hair with Granny's old brush, the carved gold leaf handle worn and the bristles yellowing. Without even looking over at me, she says, "why don't we go out to lunch?"

I smile. "Let's take a walk instead."

Mama's daily walks are a workout for anybody, walking the breezeway between buildings enough for most, but then Mama adds in the flight of stairs she insists on climbing every day. By the time Mama finishes a walk, she usually will climb back up on her bed and be asleep inside a minute. Mama, if anything, is predictable until she is not.

The one thing about taking a walk with Mama is knowing how to get out of her way and be able to hold her steady at the same time. That involves keeping your feet away from her cane and hanging tight to her left arm so she doesn't wobble. I have been on walks with her when there is more wobble than walk, and on those days I just tell her I am feeling worn out so we can cut our walks short. It's one thing to hold Mama steady, but trying to pull her up from a sitting position is a struggle. Over the last few years, Mama has lost her spring muscles and is practically dead weight to pull on unless she is sitting on a slant.

We walk across the breezeway, smiling at the other residents who look like they want Mama to stop and talk, even though Mama refuses and will only smile as she keeps moving. Mama has never been one for small talk. The rains are still beating against the windows and you can see the trees in the distance swaying like kites on a string. I know there is danger close by, but here not one person seems phased by the weather. I suppose when the majority of your days are spent inside, the outside becomes more like a picture to admire from afar.

"Mama," I say as we walk back across the breezeway. "Remember those loafers I told you about, the ones I found under my bed?"

"Loafers? You mean my old loafers? They were more comfortable than any I've had since or before." Mama stops, smiles as she looks at me, and says, "You can't give something away and expect a say in what happens to it, but if you could, I'd say you ought to take care of them."

We both laugh. "Mama, your loafers are fine."

She looks down, studies my feet for the slightest second, looking at the bedroom slippers I have borrowed while my boots dry, then starts walking. "I remember those loafers got me where I was going more years than I can remember."

Some days Mama's memory is sharp and present, and some days, like today, it's hanging on a thread. On days like these, talking about the weather and how comfortable those loafers are is as good as it needs to be. I can wonder alone why those loafers moved when they did and why they haven't moved since. There will be another day to ask Mama, wonder with her. Today is not that day. We keep walking and make our way to the lobby.

Mama buckles as we are crossing the lobby, falling as if her legs have come loose. Fortunately, I am already holding tight to that left arm and am able to reach around and hold her upright. Long enough to keep us both steady as I inch us forward to the chair a few feet away. One thing I have to commend the senior solutions folks for is that they know to fill in areas with chairs and sofas. I get Mama to the chair and ease her down. She looks white as paste and her face is as blank as a snowdrift.

My mind is swirling in a panic, afraid of what is happening to Mama and what I can do. A sharpness that takes my breath. Helplessness sends me falling through some outer space of darkness. I am trying to push myself back to reality when I hear Mama.

She lets out a long sigh. "Well, I think I'll rest for a while." Mama sits smiling, just sitting and smiling.

My mind is racing over what questions to ask, what to do. Finally, I calm my own breathing. "Mama, are you in any pain? Are you feeling sick? What happened?" I say, almost shouting, because everything we say is loud.

Mama looks at me as clear eyed as can be and says, "I said I need to rest, Pauline. That's all." As if there should not be any more discussion, she turns away and smiles at another resident, a woman probably ten years younger but struggling to guide her motorized wheelchair past us.

I start reviewing our options silently. I can call Perk to come over. I immediately scratch that off the list as the weather is still bad. I can ask for help, but looking around the lobby I see only elderly folks in worse shape than Mama. I can go find a wheelchair. The fortunate part of being at a senior solutions facility is not only the abundance of chairs and sofas but also all the empty wheelchairs. It's like being at a used car lot with free rentals everywhere. I decide on the wheelchair and tell Mama I am going to go find one.

"No, Pauline," she fusses, and I can see by the energetic way she is shaking her head that some of her strength is coming back. "I told you I just need to rest, now just sit here with me for a minute."

I have yet to bet against Mama when she is speaking up for herself, so we just sit and watch other old folks coming and going for a while. By the time I do finally pull her up to a standing position, I say, "all right Mama, no wheelchair but we are taking the elevator today, I am not going to have you falling down on the fire stairs."

She begins to say something, then gives me a little smile, her eyes lit with a twinkle.

By the time we have gotten back up to the apartment and I've helped Mama into her bed, the regular afternoon television show is on and the weather radar maps have disappeared. I have barely looked out a window since Mama collapsed, but now I can see the sun is starting to make its way through the clouds. I give Mama a kiss goodbye and turn to go.

"Don't be a stranger." she says.

I smile and turn back to say something and see her eyes have already closed.

10

Bullies

THERE IS SOMETHING FRESH AND TENDER about a clear blue sky after a storm, especially after a destructive storm like today. I haven't even walked beyond the Serenity grounds when I see one of the oak trees has fallen over the wheelchair path between the buildings. The size of that oak laying down is enough to stop your breath, and the thought of that tree tumbling to the ground sends a shudder down my spine.

No one is on the road as I walk down the few blocks to my car. I am not in the least bit self-conscious about wearing Mama's Kelly green running suit with my boots hitched up on the outside. I am not at all certain whether it is the storm's coming on so strong and then leaving just as sudden or the fact that I still have that found money unclaimed and sitting on my hall table, but by the time I reach the car and root through the contents of my pocketbook for my keys, I feel an urgency to get myself home. There is a steady stream of water flowing alongside the curb that I have to step through to reach the car door, but I am so used to the water by then I just step right in it.

I take my time making my U-turn on the empty street and driving the few blocks back to my house. I have already scanned my yard and cannot see one thing out of place, the pines still upright, the backyard free of branches. None of my neighbors seem to have any damage either, but farther down the street I can make out a flashing light and what looks to be the top of another large tree sprawled across the road. It's a good two blocks from home and I have no intention of driving down to see it. It's when I pull in the driveway that I notice the shape huddled on the steps by my front door. I put the car in park and watch Jeb sitting on the steps, studying his empty hands. The trip to Mama's had worn every bit of me out and I really just want to get back in my own home and pull off my boots. I walk all the way up to him before he even looks up.

"Jeb," I say, "Ya'll have any damage from this mess?"

"No, just a couple of branches out by the alley." He still hasn't looked up at me. Whatever is wrong is weighing heavy on the boy, and I start to worry that Jeb is back to confess that he stole the money in the first place and wants it back.

"Why don't you come in and have a cup of coffee with me." There is just no good that comes from ignoring someone in need of a shoulder, and the boy looks to need one.

Jeb is looking up past me and down at his tennis shoes and finally gives a glance my way and mumbles, "Thank you Miss Smith."

We are in the doorway practically side by side and as I step in ahead of him and plop my pocketbook on the hall table, I can see Jeb staring at the wad of money like he has just seen a ghost. There, displayed like a deck of cards across my table, sits the money in all its naked badness. Jeb stomps right past the table and the money and doesn't stop until he has stomped all the way into the kitchen. If I hadn't known the boy since he was a toddler, I would have thought him rude, but Jeb has been in my kitchen so often through the years he is practically family.

"Miss Smith, this is just a terrible thing, but I found out this morning what Mrs. Jenkins daughter's son Kenny has been doing while he has been staying with her and it is not good. Not good at all. He lives in Virginia Beach and said he was staying here all summer." Jeb has begun moving his head with a nervous twitch. "And he has gone and involved me in it because I told my mother about that money, and she saw Mrs. Jenkins at the store this morning and told her I had found all that money by your rock wall, and then Mrs. Jenkins went home and told her grandson Kenny and Kenny came to find me."

I am not even sure Jeb has taken a breath since he started talking, so I tell him to take a seat while I heat up the coffee. I'm not the best at taking a breath when I need to, but I do feel any situation can be made a little easier after you have sipped a warm drink. I keep the leftover coffee in a separate pan on the stove for just this reason. There is no need to make a fresh pot the same day when you have leftovers. I think reheated coffee is better the second time, but then I do like a strong cup.

I am bringing out the cups and sugar bowl as Jeb continues. "I was all the way at the park, lining up with two other guys to play frisbee golf, and Kenny rides over on a bicycle that looks just like the one Sam Knisley had stolen last month, rides right up to me and tells me he needs to talk to me. Right then. Miss Smith, Kenny is mean to look at, have you seen him before?"

I shake my head no, beginning to worry Jeb is going to break down and start crying right here at my kitchen table. There is not one word I know to comfort him, and I wring my hands under the table and pray Jeb collects himself. He does.

"Well he just takes me by the arm and walks me all the way back to the parking lot before he tells me his grandmother talked to my mother at the grocery store and heard I found money. Miss Smith, he told me it was his money and he threatened to mess me up if I didn't get it back to him. He said he lost it, said it must have fallen out of his pocket. And he said he knew exactly how much he lost, two thousand dollars."

I about drop the cup of coffee I have just poured Jeb and call out, "TWO THOUSAND dollars?" My eyes are about as round as saucers and I can see Jeb's are too, but he keeps going.

"Kenny tells me he's got a side business selling bicycles and he owes a guy, says that guy is coming for his cut and if I don't get it back to him he is going to send the guy over to my house. And, Miss Smith, as mean as that Kenny looks, I have a feeling that guy he is talking about is meaner."

Jeb and I are both holding our cups up to our mouths without taking a sip. Of course, I have not had time to count the money, and I know Jeb never did, but as sure as I know I am holding a strong cup of coffee I know that boy Kenny is up to no good. Not one of the neighborhood boys, including Jeb, would be involved in crime, but Kenny is from Virginia Beach and with the summer college kids and their parties down there I know all kinds of badness can take place. And I know Jeb knows that too, but he is clearly too scared to say it.

"Well," I say, "this Kenny has no business with you that I can see; after all, the money was hidden in my rock wall. That boy is lying too, Jeb. He didn't lose it, he hid it. Besides, you were just being a good neighbor. Do you want me to speak to this boy?" There is one thing I learned from Mama and a thing both Perk and I know to do, and that is not to suffer fools. And a bully is a fool. "Jeb," I say, "let's go count that money before we decide anything."

I can see Jeb clearly does not want to go anywhere near that money, but he follows me to the hallway anyway. I haven't decided on any kind of plan yet, but if that boy is right and that money adds up to two thousand dollars, I am already praying a plan is going to reveal itself to me.

We both stand in front of the hall table and I stack up the bills neatly into a tall chimney stack.

"Jeb, I want you to follow my counting and keep track of the count."

He nods and we begin. The count is up to five hundred and fifty dollars when my phone starts ringing. It is still in my pocketbook, so I stop and set the counted stack to the side.

I have just pulled out the phone and said hello when Perk says, "Are you still at Mama's?"

"No," I say, "I left her napping a while ago."

"Oh well," Perk's voice raises up as she says, "I just got another call from Laura and she says they can't find Mama. What in the good lord do those people think they need to do all day besides bother Mama?"

I am almost out of patience with this entire day. "I just left her two minutes ago napping in her bed."

"Oh don't worry, Teddy and I are headed over now," Perk says.

I let out an audible sigh and thank her. "Call me," I say, "once you find her."

I turn back to Jeb who is still standing by the table and say, "Okay, where were we?" As the counted stack mounts and the uncounted stack gets smaller, I begin to lose any confidence that this Kenny boy was wrong. We are up to $1,800 and the counted stack is a tower. I look over at Jeb and see him frowning.

"Okay," I say, "let's finish and put this stuff in a bag, Jeb." He keeps frowning at the money and I start counting again,

$1,890, $1,900, and finally, $2,005. We both look at each other then and shake our heads. That's when the plan comes to me.

When Perk and I were growing up we had a bully on our block, an older boy who was only home for summers and holidays because he went to military school the rest of the year. We heard the rumors where he set fire to a classroom at one school and he cut a boy's ear with a switchblade knife at another school, and the rumor where his father had to pay the last school extra so he didn't get kicked out. Howard George Miller III was his name, but we always just knew him as Three Eye.

Three Eye's daddy owned the Dr Pepper plant in Roanoke and had more money, I overheard Mama say one day, than was good for anyone. One summer Three Eye's daddy had a life-sized frontier fort built in their back lot, complete with a double gate that locked and a telephone pole in the middle to act as the stake to string up Indians. Three Eye was real popular the summer that frontier fort was built. All the boys on our block chose him first for cops and robbers and invited him on their campouts up Yellow Mountain.

Perk and I avoided him. He liked to call Perk Olive Oil, owing to her tall, gangly body topped off with her bright red hair, and he liked to trip me up when I was playing hopscotch. And then there was the fact that Three Eye took a liking to our dog. He didn't have a dog, and all his brothers were grown and living on their own. To be truthful, when I met Three Eye's parents, I thought they were his grandparents. His daddy was always working and his mama spent most of her time hosting bridge clubs.

Maybe that's why he stole our dog. I can look back as an adult and think up all the sad reasons Three Eye was so mean to us when we were kids, but back then there just wasn't much I loved more than our beagle, Tubby. Without a warning, one morning in July Mama let him out and he didn't come back. We were all out of the house by that night calling for him, and the next morning Mama took to the phone calling all over the block. Not one person had seen Tubby. Later it would dawn on me we hadn't seen Three Eye either.

I didn't put that together until later that next day when I was looking for him and climbed up Jefferson's Hill by Three Eye's house. I could see the gate to his frontier fort, wide open. And inside, tied to the telephone pole stake, was Tubby. Three Eye was sitting beside him, feeding him bread out of his hand. Tubby never met a food he didn't love. I can only guess that was why he hadn't barked, because from the looks of the wrappers and empty Tupperware containers, Three Eye was feeding Tubby everything from his Mama's kitchen.

I yelled "Tubby!" and ran as fast as I could over to that fort, but by the time I got there Three Eye had locked the gate tight. And if that wasn't bad enough, he started yelling, "this dog is my dog now, this is MY dog and his name is Barney. Now go away or I'll bring you in here and tie you to the stake."

I turned around and ran home. I told Mama the minute I got back to the house that Three Eye had stolen Tubby and that I was worried Three Eye wouldn't give him back to me.

"Pauline," she said, "you can't lie down and let people walk over you. You need to stand." She picked up the phone and called Three Eye's mother. I couldn't hear everything she was saying, but I did hear Mama at the end of the call saying, "Katherine, just let Howard have a dog."

I wasn't sure what to expect when Mama and I climbed the hill to the frontier fort. Somewhere along the way the idea of Three Eye being a threat to me and my Mama had gotten life sized, and I was not at all sure how we were going to wrestle Tubby away. But as we came closer to the fort, I saw Three Eye's mother standing by the gate, with one arm around

Three Eye's shoulder. She whispered something to Three Eye and he turned around and opened the gate. Tubby came running, and Mama smiled and said, "Thank you, Howard."

Mama and I walked back down the hill with Tubby running up ahead.

Not too long after that, Three Eye got a red Irish setter and called him Barney. That dog never left his side either, not even when we all played cops and robbers. I said as much to Mama one time and she said, "Well sometimes, Pauline, the dog finds the person who needs them the most."

When Three Eye went back to school that fall, I saw the gardener walking Barney in the mornings. Three Eye's parents kept that dog in their house most of the time, because whenever I did see the gardener walking him he looked like he was going to bust the leash to get free. That Thanksgiving when Three Eye came home was the first time he ever spoke to me without yelling.

The day Three Eye gave me back my dog was the day I learned to stand, and that memory includes having Mama standing right there beside me. I imagine Perk has the same sort of feeling about that. We both learned from early on that we would always stand, that being a victim was the same as suffering fools, and as Mama's girls we just did not do that. And that we would always stand together. Family is who stands with you.

"Jeb," I say now, "let's take a walk."

If there is one thing that will set a bully on his back heels faster than a knockout punch it is bringing their mama in on it. Or, in this case, their granny. I have my pocketbook in one hand and the bag of money in the other as I walk with Jeb up to Mrs. Jenkins house. She lives on the other side of the alley on Clinton. I can see her black Honda Fit out front. Mrs. Jenkins is retired from the UPS and rarely leaves her house. She told me once that after all those years of delivering people's packages, she is happy to just stay in her own home most of the time.

Jeb and I walk up to the door and ring the bell. I have already discussed the plan. We are here to speak to Mrs. Jenkins. If Kenny is here as well, we will let him speak up in the presence of his grandmother. Mrs. Jenkins comes to the door wearing a tired looking housecoat and pink terry cloth slippers. It is only mid-afternoon, but I suppose if you are not leaving your house and the only person you are expecting to see is your grandson, it's enough.

She does seem surprised to see us, but I just step in and get down to business. "Mrs. Jenkins, Jeb here had a run in with Kenny today and I am involved in a real coincidental way. Do you mind if we come in?"

She is looking at us and not saying a thing, but she nods and we walk into a dark paneled hallway. The curtains in the living room are drawn shut and I can see the blue light from the television in her den bouncing shapes across the hall.

"KENNY," she shouts out. She is still staring at us but calling out again and again until we hear a door open upstairs and a shuffle of feet down the steps. If looks could kill, both Jeb and I would already be six feet under from the expression Kenny has when he sees us.

"What are you doing here?" he says to Jeb. Kenny has not given me one glance.

"Mrs. Jenkins, Kenny here told Jeb he lost two thousand dollars by my back wall and threatened Jeb if he didn't return it. So you can imagine my surprise when I found that very amount hidden behind a loose stone in my wall. Seems to me hiding money in a wall is far from losing it. Kenny must really be saving his pennies to have so much cash lying around. For the life of me, though Mrs. Jenkins, I cannot fathom why he would hide it inside my back wall?"

Mrs. Jenkins is looking at me and Kenny is looking at Jeb and Jeb is staring at the floor. I smile at Mrs. Jenkins and say, "I just thought you should know."

I hand her over the bag of money and thank her for her time. Kenny is still glaring at Jeb and I continue smiling at Mrs. Jenkins as I nudge Jeb out the door. We are halfway to the street when we hear Mrs. Jenkins shouting, "DO NOT LIE TO ME."

For the first time today, I see Jeb smile.

There is something to be said about holding on to memories from your childhood, the good ones and the bad, because the thing about reaching the advanced years is you get to look back on all of them and see them all through older eyes. It is not likely I would have believed you if you had told me sixty years ago that I would be standing up to a young bully by bringing his Granny into the mix, but I have a feeling that years from now Jeb is going to look back and see our little walk to the Jenkins house as one of his standing up moments. Memories don't ever go away, memories like me and my Mama watching Three Eye back down. Memories just sit back and wait until you need to bring them to the surface and draw on them. That alone is enough to make me smile today.

11

Same As Always

JEB AND I SAY GOOD-BYE AT THE CORNER and I walk back to
the house. Today is mostly gone. My list of To Do's started
and ended with my trip to Mama's. Everything since has been
pure happenstance. Now that I am home and heating up a
chicken pot pie for dinner, there is not a thing I want to do
but put on a nightgown and turn on the television. I could sit
and watch Law and Order reruns all night and be perfectly
happy. Perk hasn't called back to say where she found Mama
yet, which tells me Mama is fine. Jeb practically skipped
away when we parted. You forget what the weight of a bully
targeting you can do to a body, until you see a youngster like
Jeb free of them.

When my phone starts ringing just at the critical point
in the Law and Order episode where Olivia figures out who
the child molester is, I answer it as if I know exactly what
is coming, even though I could not have known, could not
have imagined what was coming next. Except that of all days,
this day has started out like any other and has proceeded to
unwrap itself with one surprise after another.

"Hello," I say, holding the television remote mute button,
ready to unmute just as soon as the phone call ends. I could

recite what Detective Olivia Benson was saying word for word, I have seen the episode so many times.

"Hello?" I say again. I can hear a song playing in the background, something country, nothing I can place.

"Pauline Smith?" a woman says in a gravelly voice that sounds just full of cigarette smoke.

"Yes," I answer, ready to say no thank you to whatever the woman is selling and get back to my show.

"PAULINE Smith? This is Bob Redford's wife calling."

"Who?"

It is one thing to have a stranger call you at night and entirely another consideration to have a stranger call who knows your name. And what is Bob's ex-wife from South Hill doing calling me? If there is ever a time to call me and expect any portion of understanding, it is not in the evenings after 8 pm when the network shows are at their best.

"Excuse me?" I say, straining to keep a level tongue. "Are you his ex-wife from South Hill?"

"No I am not, I am Sally Redford his current and only wife from South Hill and now living in Richmond, Virginia."

That sends me bolt upright in bed. Any weariness from the day has left and I am wide eyed staring at my phone in disbelief.

"Who?" I try to calm my breathing but give up and just breathe as deep as I can. The automatic reflex to block out what I have just heard before it can hurt me kicks in and her next words come at me in a blur of words and phrases.

"Sally Redford. I told you already. And my husband thinks it is perfectly all right to talk to me about his friend Pauline who reminds him of his Mama. As if that kind of talk is ever going to be all right when a wife has finally gotten her husband to retire and spend time with her. Well, Pauline, guess what?"

I am unnerved that this woman continues to call me by my first name when I know absolutely nothing about her. "What?"

My body has already started slumping, a coldness taking over me like after Daddy died, and Carleton died, and Reggie went to jail. Shock never seems to find me prepared.

"Instead of taking a cooking class to celebrate his retirement he would rather go back to his old mail route and visit a woman who reminds him of his Mama." Her gravel voice sounds like a snarl.

"The one at Northbridge mall?" I say before I can stop myself. Perk had just been telling me about a new cooking class starting up at Northbridge mall the other day.

"None of your goddamn business, bitch. Did my Bob tell you about that, too? Because no shriveled up old bitch is taking my husband."

Sally Redford is breathing so hard through the phone I am beginning to wonder if I should hang up and call 911 for her, but right now I am under attack. I have already decided this woman is no one I ever want to meet or speak to again, but until I can say my piece I am not hanging up. She is, as Perk would say, an emotional basket case, if the shrill tone of her voice is any indication. She is speaking so loudly I probably could have left the TV sound going and still heard her ranting, and so I hold the phone in front of me without even putting it on speaker and listen to the rest of what she is saying.

"And I don't know what you said to my husband, bitch, but it stops now. It stops." Her voice shakes a little at the end, almost like her rage is going to spill out over the phone.

My head is spinning like I have vertigo and I scare myself, wondering if I am crazy, if this is really happening, if my feelings for Bob and his for me have all just been in my own head. She keeps on breathing hard, cussing now in a whisper. Before she can say another thing, I sit up straighter in the bed, feeling a warmth spreading through me. I might be crazy, but the woman is just plain rude. And then I remember. The phone calls, the hang ups.

"Mrs. Redford, have you been calling me and just hanging up?"

"What if I did, bitch?"

This woman has gone off the rails, and I have had enough of her. "Now you listen here, Mrs. Bob Redford, Sally Redford or whatever your name is. You will not speak to me that way, and, not that I care one minute what you think, I had no idea Bob was married. And, even now that I know he is married, I see nothing wrong with sharing a conversation and a cup of coffee with a married man. He is just a friend, for heaven's sake."

Even as I am saying this and standing my ground, my brain is trying to understand how this is all happening, how my heart is hurting for a man I clearly do not know, how that hurt is spreading inside me, even with all the protections I put in place to keep it away. Nobody gets through life without pain, that's a pure fact.

More shouting, and then I hear her stammering on the line, slinging a curse word under her breath. "Goddamn bitch."

Raising my voice a little higher, enough that both cats look up at me puzzled, I say, "And as far as Bob is concerned, good Lord, why don't you talk to him? Anyone rude enough to call up a stranger at night and put the blame anywhere but where it belongs is in need of something I can't give you. Don't you ever call me again."

I hang up the phone, not waiting for a reply, unmute the television volume, and stare at Olivia Benson as she hears the judge raise the gavel and say, "Guilty."

The cats are sitting on the edge of the bed, looking at me as if I have just turned my head around three times. No amount of deep breathing is going to calm me down now, so I get up, put on my robe, and go out to the kitchen. The viciousness in that woman's voice is still in my ears. Violence has never come close to my door, but hearing Sally Redford tonight, it feels like it is creeping in, and I feel myself shudder. I'm pulled back as I replay it all in my mind. Bob, married, and not saying a word. Bob, coming courting, and lying with every smile he gave me. I move in short halting steps, the pain welling up inside me, and an old pang of loneliness takes hold.

There is heartbreak that comes when a loved one dies, and it is pure and tragic and wholesome in the way it hurts, like a wound cut clean. You will recover from feelings that are pure in their loss. And then there is the heartbreak that comes when you've been wronged, and bamboozled, and cheated on. And that hurts just as much, and twice as long, until you have finished with the anger. And you will recover. Then there is this surprising heartbreak that comes with a loss you hadn't known would mean so much, and that hurts long enough to recognize how little you knew and how much you cared, and you will recover. But not until you forgive yourself, and that can take the longest. Knowing that only comes with time.

For the life of me I don't know where to put my sore heart tonight. I am struggling with the idea of liking someone so much before getting to know who he is, and the idea that my heart can be hurt again after all these years of protection. And there just aren't any good answers. I am what you would call a light drinker, a glass of wine at a social gathering or at home if there is leftover in the refrigerator. I've already drunk the leftover book club Chardonnay, but the brandy I use for Christmas eggnog is sitting up on the top shelf. I use a kitchen chair to reach it. Sitting down and pouring myself a glass, I take a sip and feel the warming down my throat spread. I let out a sigh that sounds more like a sob.

Bob. Who never talked about himself or anybody much, and when he did he talked about the ex-wife back in South Hill. Why would he lie about that? And never once mentioning that I remind him of his mother. And if he had, I am not so sure I would have taken that as a compliment.

I try to pick apart my conversations with Bob, scrutinize every word he's said to me, and realize there was not one where he talked about Richmond or what he did here when he was not delivering mail. No ring on his finger. No talking about being married. Currently. For all his familiarity, I am realizing he is a stranger to me. I take another sip of the brandy. My heart is sore and my anger is heating my blood, and all I can concentrate on is that I have gone and done it again, despite all my years of staying away from romance, in spite of all my locks on my heart, I've gone and done it again. I take another sip of brandy. The brandy bottle is becoming a caramel colored blur as I continue to sip. The room feels as empty as my heart.

It seems like a minute ago that Bob was in this very kitchen. What was it he said? *I'll see you soon.* I hadn't thought anything of it other than how casual and comfortable that had sounded. If truth be told I had already begun to label Robert Redford as a selfless man, not a narcissist like Reggie or a boy destined to be swallowed by his own recklessness like Carleton. I feel my body heating up with brandy and anger. One thing is sure, I decide, if Bob Redford shows his face here again he will be holding a conversation with me from the other side of the front door. I can hear Mama as plain as if she is here beside me, saying, "do not suffer fools." A liar is the biggest fool of all.

But there's another truth, and that's that I am as angry at myself for letting my heart be hurt as I am at Bob for lying. I shake my head at the misery I am feeling over a relationship that's barely started and how quick I opened my heart to him. I walk back to the bedroom, too tired to stir up any more feelings, too dizzy from the brandy to think another thought. I crawl under my sheets, mumbling, "No I do not suffer fools."

The next morning, I wake late and see the sun shining through the bedroom curtains. I wake unsettled, as if I have missed something of importance, or have stepped onto the top rung of a ladder, unbalanced. Last night seems about as foreign as watching a movie with subtitles. It is a fact that Bob's wife called me, and even though that is becoming more important the longer I am awake, the one thought walking with me on my way to the kitchen is how nice Sammy and his mother had been, offering me the ride to Mama's. That yesterday had started out with kindness. Yesterday, a day too full to hold much of it at all. Yesterday, I think, *that was a day*.

As I shuffle past the hallway and glance over at the front door, I see, again, the empty space beside the door, where the loafers should be. My head is calling out for coffee and an ibuprofen as I say softly, "About time." My brandy hangover is already mixed in with the soreness I feel in my heart, but still, under it all, I feel a comfort, knowing where I will find those missing loafers, and hear myself mutter, "I am going to be alright."

It takes three ibuprofen and two cups of coffee before I am ready, but when I do finally lower myself down to the floor and look under the bed, my cheek pressing into the scatter rug, my eyes fill with tears. I lay still and begin to let out the little droplets softly, not willing to give Bob the benefit of a good cry, cradling one arm on the side of my head, and reaching in towards the headboard with the other. I can see the loafers in the shadows, backlit in their glow. I feel for all the world held and comforted by them resting there. I will tell all of this to Mama, I think.

"Nobody in their right mind would have called you up like that," Perk says, later that morning, when I tell her about the phone call from Sally Redford. "Nobody. That woman is off her rocker."

Perk has stopped by on her way to Mama's to drop off groceries. I am never surprised to see Perk. She is more comfortable on the go and dropping in on me, Mama, her kids, and sometimes even her neighbors than any one of us. I am comfortable in my own skin but dropping in on folks has never been my choice. I go when I am invited but I always call first if I decide to visit a person. Not Perk.

"That woman is clearly crazy, but Perk, I just feel awful that I like Bob so much and I don't know him at all. I feel like I am as crazy as she is. Like I have just been living it all in my own head."

"Nonsense. Pauline, we both know it takes one look to fall for somebody. Some of us get lucky we are looking at the right one, and most of us don't. That man knew what he was doing. He put his eye on you the minute he showed up at your door. Any one of us would have fallen for all that attention, Pauline."

I sigh, Perk's words washing like a balm over me. I am relieved to see her. The thought of talking my way through all the events of yesterday without the benefit of sitting face to face would have been exhausting. As it is, we sit at the kitchen table, me sipping my third cup of coffee for the day and Perk on her fourth. I have always found that whatever the circumstances, Perk has a knack for simplifying and translating into something easy to digest. She gets that from Mama.

The time I showed up at her door crying because Reggie had been put in jail for selling drugs, Perk sat me down.

"Well," she'd said, "it was either Reggie going to jail or Mama was going to have you committed. There were signs, Pauline. I'm not saying you didn't want to see them, but when the police know what your boyfriend is up to and you don't, I'd say there is at the very least an honesty problem."

It had taken months of feeling sorry for myself after Reggie went to jail before I woke up and smelled the coffee, as Mama would say. Perk had called his drug arrest divine intervention.

Now as I'm reciting what Bob's wife said, I can see that look Perk is giving me, the one saying, *Here we go again, the one saying I love you, I'm here for you.*

"I just feel like a fool, Perk. I didn't even see it coming. All of a sudden my mailman's stirring my heart with feelings I haven't had since Reggie. I can't believe I liked him so much and didn't even know him. I'm not sure if I'm madder that I let him hurt me or that I was such a blind fool."

"Pauline, the man was throwing all his attention your way. In my mind he is as crazy as that wife of his, if it's true. And we don't know."

"I think we do, Perk. That woman might have been crazy, but she sounded true."

I roll my eyes. "I mean, yes, of course it was flattering, I know once a man starts bringing on attention and acting so nice, you get comfortable with that attention real quick. And it hurts thinking how nice he was to me and how good that made me feel. It hurts my heart a lot. But last night, that woman sounding crazy and angry, pouring it all out on me, calling me a bitch, well I just don't have any use at all for that kind of drama. I'm too old, Perk, for that nonsense. I might be a damn fool, but even fools get to have their say." As I say it, I know it's true. I'm going to have to look at Bob a different way, through the rear view.

Perk is smiling, and even before I ask her why, she says, "Pauline, you are beginning to sound just like Mama."

"Except I was the fool this time," I say, shaking my head, but already feeling a little lighter.

"Oh, did I tell you where we found Mama yesterday?" Changing the subject's always been one way Perk will let you know she thinks a problem's done. "Teddy found her on the fire stairs, between the fifth and sixth floors, leaned up against the stair railing, just sitting quietly. When Mama saw him, she looked up with that little smile of hers and said…"

We both say it at the same time. "What took you so long?" Mama says that just about any time now we go to see her, like she knows we will be there, sooner or later, even if she is stuck on the fire steps and can't get up. Mama's faith is stubborn and true.

Perk and I start laughing then, and before I know it the ache is fading, thoughts of Bob and Sally Redford are dissolving, disappearing into an unfortunate memory from a day that's passed. My heart's still aching, but sitting here with Perk, letting all of that ugliness out, as if a chorus of Mama and Perk are already singing, "you are going to be alright", I feel a lightness alongside the heart. My family support has always been the fastest road to recovery.

I decide to ride over to Mama's with Perk. Today is a good day to have Perk for company. Any back-peddling thoughts I might have about Bob can be smashed with just one look from Perk, and that, I figure, is reason enough to go with her. I collect my pocketbook from the hallway and slip on the loafers. Once I finally picked myself and the loafers up from the bedroom, I put them right back here, in the hallway, where they ought to be. For a moment I can see them in Mama's old house, by the kitchen door, leading out to the stoop, where Mama kept them all those years while Perk and I were growing up. Same loafers, thinner soles, all these years later. I slip them on and feel grounded, safe, protected.

Perk is already out ahead of me, halfway to her car talking to me like I am right there beside her. I have never known if she does that because she is so caught up in what she is saying or because she just assumes I am going to be stuck to her like glue whenever we are together. I do know if you don't keep up, Perk will leave without you and keep talking as if you are right there with her. And most of the time Perk is saying something you want to hear, or need to hear, or don't even know you need to hear until later when you remember what she was saying.

12

It Could Be Worse

WHEN PERK AND I WERE LITTLE we used to visit the relatives every Christmas morning after we opened presents while Mama and Daddy had their coffee and Granny and Grandaddy walked across the alley for breakfast. After we visited all the relatives, and there were many, on both Mama and Daddy's sides of the family, we went back to Granny and Grandaddy's for a big lunch with our cousins and Aunt Eleanor and Uncle Bart and Aunt Florence. By the time we got to go home, Perk and I were usually too tired to play with any of our toys. There was never a thought that you wouldn't go visit the relatives. That was what you did. And even after all the relatives had died, including Mama's sisters Eleanor and Florence and Granny and Granddaddy and Auntie, the thought never left us that you visit the family that are left, even if you hardly know them.

I suppose that was why when I told the women at book club about Mama, how Perk and I checked in on her daily and bought the groceries and made sure she didn't burn the place down cooking her own dinner, I didn't pay any mind to their blank stares and comments about putting her in the assisted living wing. Even though all of the little irritations of becoming more caretaker than daughter got under my skin, there was never any thought that I would just send Mama somewhere she didn't want to go. Not until it was necessary, not until she was a danger to herself. Perk didn't care one bit what other people thought about that. I cared some, but I cared about doing right for Mama more.

Even though Mama is going to be 97 soon, Perk and I both know we are living this life right now with Mama as one of Management by Crisis; we leave things alone until Mama has an accident or falls sick, and we let her keep on living the way she wants to live until she can't. Something will happen someday, but until it does, we buy the groceries and fix the television remote and check in on Mama. Every day. Family takes care of family.

As Perk is pulling up to Mama's building, still talking about the nerve of Sally Redford, we see the ambulance out front. This is nothing new. It is a rare morning when I don't hear the fire truck racing by my house, on the way to put out someone's breakfast fire in Mama's building or in one of the other buildings at Serenity. And the ambulances too. As Perk says, "Well they are all OLD, Pauline, they are going to fall and need oxygen and, let's face it, die."

That bothered me when we first moved Mama here. I suspected the reason for all the ambulances and fire trucks was due to neglect on the part of management. But the longer Mama has been here, I've realized it is just the price of independence for the elderly. And until the bad days are every day, we should all just let them be and live the way they want to. Like Mama.

Perk steps out of the car and is still talking about the crazy Sally Redford, and I am locking my door and trying to catch up to her even though the puddles from yesterday's deluge are more like tidal pools, soaking through my loafers, when we both see her. Up ahead, laid out on a stretcher with a blanket from her bed laid across her, and a big gash across one eye, blood all the way down her face. I can't tell if she is unconscious or dead but there is no question that this is our Mama being wheeled out of the building.

Perk appears at her side without even taking a stride, it seems, and I am just frozen, staring at Mama and the two EMT's beside her. It is true what they say that the big shocking moments come at you like a dream. I suppose that is to coat the nerves, make sure you don't absorb it all too soon. As it was, I got myself over to Mama and held her hand while Perk found out the facts. She had fallen. She was conscious. She was going to the hospital. We could meet her there.

There have been plenty of times when Mama has fallen and we have stopped anyone from taking her to the hospital. But those have been the little falls, the tumbles that she has taken that don't mean anything but a bit of rest. Today, Perk doesn't say one word of argument to the EMT's, doesn't even ask why they did not call her. We can both see Mama is full of pain, her cheekbone bloodied. Perk kisses her and I do too and then they load her into the back of the ambulance.

I don't say a word until we are back in Perk's car.

"This is bad."

Perk, pulling the car out and lining it up behind the ambulance, looks over at me and says, "It could be worse."

There are times when I think my sister is insensitive, and there are times when I think she says the only thing that matters. Today, it's the latter. My rush to fear Mama is dying is squashed with those simple words—*it could be worse.*

We arrive at the hospital and park and find Mama in an exam room, already being triaged and tended to by nurses who look too young to be working at anything but babysitting, and a doctor so handsome and young I could swear I am watching an episode of General Hospital.

Perk and I both sit by the door and watch. There are times when you advocate, and times when you sit back and wait. I don't know if that comes from years of listening to Grandaddy talk about the patients he saw in his ER, or if it comes from knowing emergency medicine is mostly about taking care of the immediate. The part of medicine I have a problem with is the rest of it, the expensive tests and unnecessary procedures and all out scare tactics some doctors seem to use without even batting an eye, no regard for the patient, just the protocols and procedures, as if every patient was identical, the same age, same condition. So for now we wait and watch.

The emergency room doctor orders Mama wheeled out for x-rays. "The right upper arm," he says, "appears to be broken." He tells us they will call in the plastic surgeon and the orthopedist once she gets back.

When you are a worrier like I am, you tend to believe a doctor when they tell you what your mother needs. You put your trust in them. Perk, on the other hand, worries very little and does not trust any doctors until they tell her the facts. She is a woman born of action.

She straightens her back before she says, "You do know our mother is almost 97 years old? There will not be a need for plastic surgery or orthopedics unless she cannot breathe. Can she breathe, doctor?" Perk is looking at him with kindness and steel all boiled into one expression. If you didn't know her you would see the kindness. As it was, I could see the steel.

The young doctor, looking very surprised, says, "Why yes, but that is going to be a deep scar along her cheekbone. I am not the orthopedist, but my guess is he will want to go in and repair bone on the upper arm, as well."

Perk's expression has lost most of the kindness and now appears to be mostly steel, even to the handsome young doctor. Smiling, she looks at him directly and says, "I am the durable and medical power of attorney for our mother and there will be no surgery, plastics or orthopedics. Our mother is almost 97 years old and I will not have you put her under anesthesia for a scar or a broken bone. That arm can scar over, and besides, she is not planning on doing handstands."

There is not much you can do when you come up against a determined Perk. When she was a child, she was called Carrot Top because her hair was practically orange, but by the time she was in college she was known as Big Red, after her hair settled into a bright red auburn and her will became unbreakable. The young doctor types something on his iPad and says, "Yes, ma'am. I have made a note in her chart."

The look on his face reminds me of James when he was young and did something wrong and Perk would send him to the corner for a timeout. The beat look on his face would make me want to hug him and tell him it would be alright. Seeing this young doctor looking so beat makes me want to do the same. I move in front of Perk so he faces me, and I say, "Thank you so much for your care. We appreciate it so much." The doctor frowns at his iPad, almost like my appreciation has pained him. He looks up and nods to me, then tells us he will be back and disappears down the hall, practically running as he turns a corner.

The time you spend in hospitals is not the same as normal time you spend anywhere else. It passes in big chunks and at the same time slower than waiting for Christmas in July. Perk leaves to pick up Teddy from the car repair shop and hands me Mama's Medicare and Blue Cross supplemental IDs, with clear instructions not to let them schedule surgery,

As far as I can tell, there is nothing to do but wait. And wait. Even though it is eighty degrees outside, the exam room is several degrees cooler than comfortable. My loafers are still wet and the skimpy cotton of my pants and short sleeved shirt are no match for the chill. I suppose they do that on purpose for the patients, but it might be more important to the families waiting. I have a hard time thinking about anything other than how cold I am.

I walk out to the hallway to get some circulation moving and see, coming around the same corner the doctor disappeared around, Sammy Engels and his mother. She has one arm around Sammy's shoulder and her head is looking down. I can't tell her expression, but Sammy is looking straight ahead, like he is in some kind of trance. The sadness surrounding the both of them is palpable. Sammy's eyes focus on me and slowly I see the light coming back in his eyes. His mother looks up and nods to me like it is the most natural thing in the world to run into me here, in the emergency room, in this hospital. "Hey Pauline."

"Hey Sandy. Hey Sammy." I nod to the both of them, smile slightly.

Sandy leans towards me but keeps her arm around Sammy's shoulder. "Sammy's grandmother died today." Her eyes are filled with tears, even though I know this is the ex-husband's mother and the woman she clearly is not fond of. The grandmother she knows her son loves dearly.

"I am so sorry." There is just nothing more to say.

Sammy and his mother both nod again and continue down the hall. Come next spring, I'm going to get Sammy to start mowing my grass with Jeb. Maybe he can start off trimming. Let him take over once Jeb goes to college. Make sure he's not breaking into any more houses with his high school friends. Maybe even get him to shovel snow with Jeb.

I walk back into the exam room. The one thing I haven't realized I count on is Mama's smile. When she is rolled back in from the x-ray with her face still scrunched up in pain, and no sign of any relief, I begin to panic. You do not want anyone you love to be in pain, and when you are a worrier there is nothing else on your mind. Without Perk here to calm me down, the best I can do is keep her words close. It could be worse. I stand beside Mama and hold her hand and wait.

13

Stand

THE ONE THING ABOUT GROWING UP with a Grandaddy
who was also a surgeon was that you got to know the person
before you understood the power of the job. Perk and I knew
our Grandaddy to be loving and fair, and for a long time I
thought all doctors were like that. We listened to his stories
at Sunday lunch about sewing up stomach punctures and
setting bones and telling a mother her son was dead, all while
watching him pour heavy cream over his applesauce. Later,
when the hospital was trying to get him to retire, so that his
vote wouldn't count against bringing on the HCA, we watched
him boil over in anger and yell at no one in particular. Even
before I turned ten years old, I could see my Grandaddy as a
person, flawed like anybody else and not perfect.

I understood Grandaddy's competence as a doctor, even
if I could not have put that into words. I knew this from
experience, after I ran down the stairs in our house and out
the front door by pushing my arm through the glass storm
door. Mama came running from the kitchen when she
heard my screams and carried me straight across the alley
to Granny and Grandaddy's house. Grandaddy, home for
lunch, laid me out on their bed, took out sterilized scissors,
and before I could work up my fear, had snipped off the dead

skin, sewed up my right arm in little patchwork quilt stitches where the glass had cut the skin, and patted me on the head. The whole procedure was over before I knew it, and Granny was handing me a popsicle.

Mama is admitted to the hospital and given fluids and pain medicine and provided a soft cast for her arm. Perk and I take turns sitting with her, and it happens to be my turn the morning after her fall when a group of doctors step into the room. They arrive in such a flurry you would think they were homing pigeons, swooping in and gathering around the bed. By now Mama has been on pain medicine long enough to relax, and she greets them with a smile.

The lead doctor introduces himself and starts explaining the surgery he has scheduled for Mama that afternoon. He smiles at Mama, glances at the chart he holds, and continues talking so fast I can only catch every third or fourth word. I do hear surgery though, and I wonder if he has come into the wrong room, is talking about the wrong patient, because Perk couldn't have been clearer with instructions for no surgery. As I listen, I start turning all kinds of red, knowing I am going to have to repeat every last one of Perk's directives.

"We are refusing any surgeries. My sister has the power of attorney. Do I need to call her?" I say without looking back at Mama. There is just no use in explaining to these doctors the truth of this; that if Mama can't use her arm, she can't hold a cane and walk on her own, and if she can't walk on her own, her mind is going to fade all the way gone. The bone can scar over, the arm can be set with a soft cast. Grandaddy had set Granny's arm that way one time when she slipped on the ice in the driveway. Besides, not one of the doctors mentions the dangers of anesthesia for an elderly woman in her nineties.

Perk and I have advocated for Mama's healthcare ever since she turned eighty-five and started falling. Perk, Teddy, and I were home for the Fourth of July, sitting in the living room. Teddy was telling us about the house James was thinking about buying down in Charlotte. I noticed I hadn't seen Mama.

"Where's Mama?" I asked.

"I think she's upstairs, reading." Perk had replied.

We both looked at each other at the same time and jumped up. When we were all home, Mama made a point to see our faces every chance she got. We started looking around the house, upstairs, in the basement, and finally, Teddy found her, down by the alley, sitting beside the trashcan. She had fallen and couldn't get herself up.

"What took you so long?" she had asked him. Her face was the color of a ripe tomato on the vine.

Teddy helped her back into the house and Perk took her blood pressure. It was down so low she should have been passed out. An hour later, Mama was rested and ready to go out to dinner. I wanted to call in sick to work and stay in Roanoke with Mama, but she wouldn't have it.

"Go home, Pauline. I'm fine. I just stumbled and couldn't get a grip."

Perk had called her primary care doctor once she got back to Richmond and found out he had put her on a cholesterol medicine the year before. She was irate." Who puts an eight-four-year old woman on cholesterol medicine? She can't live long enough for her arteries to clog."

Teddy did some research and found out one of the side effects of cholesterol medicine can be muscle atrophy. We took Mama off that medicine as soon as we found out. Perk drove to Roanoke and took Mama to a new doctor, who did a run of tests and ended up saying Mama was fine except also ought to get off her blood pressure medicine.

When Perk told me that, both of us knew that most doctors just don't know how to care for the elderly. Most of our trust in doctors went right out the window after that.

I drove to Roanoke the next weekend to check on Mama. She had already made plans with her friend Mildred to go to the Roanoker for dinner, so I joined them. As we were sipping our glasses of Chardonnay, Mildred asked Mama if she'd fallen lately. Mama shot her a look and said, "Hush," but it was too late.

"Did you know she fell last weekend, Mildred?" I said, feeling a jolt of alarm running through me.

"No sweetie, but I've been falling for years. I told Eloise how to get herself up. She's got that banister she can pull herself up on. You just need something to pull up on."

Mama looked over at me like a child caught with a hand in the cookie jar.

"Mama, how long have you been falling?"

"Oh, not long, Pauline. Now let's order. Mildred, didn't you have the fried chicken last time?"

I drove back to Richmond that Sunday fretting over what could happen if Mama fell and hit her head or fell and couldn't get up. By the time I got home, I had all but decided Mama needed to move. I called Perk that night, and as I was telling her what I thought, that Mama should move to the retirement village some of her friends had moved to, Perk stopped me.

"Pauline, you will cut the heart out of her if you make her move. You have to decide, what kind of relationship do you want with your mother? Contentious, antagonistic, or respectful of her wishes? She wants to live in her house, and as long as she can, I respect her choice."

"I just worry she's going to hurt herself."

"Well, don't. Until something happens, Mama is happy. Think about that, Pauline."

We hung up and I put aside my worry. After that, though, I made a point to drive to Roanoke every month for a weekend, sometimes more than once a month, depending how worried I felt.

The entire group of doctors standing around Mama now are as stone-faced as one of those Confederate generals out on Monument Avenue. The lead doctor looks like he would give about anything to be anywhere but in this room. I see all of the doctor's eyes on me. A portrait of the Confederate general Jeb Stuart stares at me through the open door from the far side of the hallway. I glare back at that group of doctors and don't say another word. I am standing. In our family, we stand. As uncomfortable as I am feeling, I stand.

Every last one of those doctors all look down at their iPads like they are studying for a test. The lead doctor finally speaks up. "Mrs. Smith," he says to Mama, "We want to take very good care of you, and surgery will help give you back your range of motion in that right shoulder." He smiles so wide I decide he is grinning when he adds, "But if you choose not to have the surgery we will discharge you once your vitals are normal." He speaks to Mama like she is a child, then looks over at me and the smile fades. "Ms. Smith, your mother will need adequate care once she is discharged." He says this like it is a bad thing.

"Of course, she will be taken care of," I say. This doctor has some nerve suggesting Mama won't get the care she needs. I glare at him.

The group of them turn around and leave, swooping out of that room as quickly as they entered. I look over at Mama then and see she is already sound asleep. I look over at the portrait of Jeb Stuart and let out a sigh. Enough battles for one day.

The thing about an old person living on their own is that they have to be mobile in order for that to work. You can check in on them and buy the groceries and prepare the meals, but they have to be able to move around. Otherwise it is round-the-clock care and that is just too expensive for most of us to afford. I know that there just isn't a way to get Mama back to her apartment and leave her alone, not with a broken arm. Perk and I have to find a place for Mama to rehabilitate. And soon.

After the doctors leave I go out to the hall and call Perk. "Those doctors came by. They are going to discharge Mama as soon as her blood pressure steadies." I am trying to whisper but having a hard time keeping my voice low, my worry for where Mama goes next and the confrontation with the doctors still stirring my nerves. "They came in here trying to schedule her for surgery, Perk. We have got to find a place for Mama, but I can take care of her until we do." The words sit like a lump in my throat.

"Pauline, the last time Mama stayed with you she practically drove you crazy. Have you forgotten driving over to my house to say that Mama was starting to even make the cats nervous? And with our two-story, you know Mama can't come stay with us and climb those stairs."

Every time I think Mama should come live with me again, I remember adjusting from living alone to taking care of Mama, preparing healthy meals and getting her to take her medicines. Mama never liked cooking. When Hester was still living, she would come cook for Mama once a week, even after her arthritis took hold, well into her seventies. The two of them were as close as sisters and Mama went to visit Hester up until her death. Once Hester finally moved in with her daughter and officially retired, Mama went from eating home cooked meals to frozen dinners and prepared foods from

Kroger's. Once Mama moved in with me, and I would try to make her a chicken dinner from scratch, she would turn up her nose and say, "What's this?"

"It's dinner, Mama." Even in the first week I couldn't hold my tongue when she got snippy with me.

Those first weeks when Mama stayed with me, after her fall in Roanoke, I didn't tell her she was moving to Richmond for good. I kept saying, "As soon as you mend, Mama," when she asked when she was going home. I had lined up the therapy and cooked the meals and listened to the groans she let out when she was trying to get comfortable in a chair or on the bed. If Perk had heard those groans, she would have made light of it. I was the opposite, my nerves hanging on every groan until I had made her comfortable.

It was Perk who found the apartment at Serenity, and when I told her that I wasn't sure it was time, that Mama was still in some pain, she had said, "Well Pauline, the woman is almost 96, of course she is going to be in discomfort. Nobody is going to feel good with a broken shoulder bone. And if she doesn't leave your house soon, she's never going to let us move her."

Those weeks living with Mama had been a trial, but I got through them. As you do when it comes to family. I know Perk is right though. I just couldn't take care of Mama again and take care of myself at the same time. We had talked about what we would do if Mama could not live on her own, but we didn't have any set plan.

"But we don't have a plan", I say now. "And until we do, where else is she going? She will drive me crazy, but I can do it again." Perk heaves a sigh and I do too.

I drive home and spend the afternoon looking through the phone book, writing down phone numbers for rehabilitation centers, then clean my spare bedroom and put fresh sheets and fluffed up pillows on the bed. I add to the grocery list on the hall table foods that Mama likes. Perk calls me that evening and tells me she has called five rehabs and not one of them has a bed for Mama. I sleep through fretful dreams and wake up irritated. I am beginning to feel overwhelmed, and Mama hasn't even come to stay with me yet.

The only good news about this hospital stay is that the social worker, Belinda, helps us arrange for a rehabilitation stay at the nursing home nearby. She walks into Mama's room the next day. I am sitting beside Mama's bed, telling Mama about the new Jodi Picoult book I am reading for book club.

"Mrs. Smith," Belinda says, smiling and looking directly at Mama, "The doctors tell me you are going to be discharged tomorrow."

My stomach drops with the word *discharge* and I feel like I have been punched. We don't have anywhere to take Mama. Unless she goes home with me.

Belinda looks over at me and smiles wide. "I found a bed for your mother just down the street, at Gentle Healings." Mama smiles, her eyes vacant.

"Oh that is wonderful, Belinda." I feel my stomach settle, my neck muscles loosen. This pencil-skinny woman with graying black hair is here to save us, and she has. This news is like a cold wash on a hot day. I call Perk and pass the phone to Belinda and while the two of them review insurance and paperwork I sit beside Mama, holding her hand and smiling along with her.

The day we are to move Mama from the hospital to the nursing home is gray and raining. Perk, Teddy, and I sit with Mama for what seems like half the afternoon waiting on the discharge. Teddy checks his phone every two minutes and

Perk flips through a Time magazine and I pace the room. Mama sleeps in the wheelchair wearing her nightgown, with her raincoat draped loosely around the sling holding her arm in place. Finally, a young nurse comes in with the discharge papers.

"Your Mama is just a delight," she says. "She tells me every time I come in the room I have a beautiful smile." The young nurse laughs, then adds, "She told me yesterday you were coming to take her back to Roanoke."

I feel my heart tug. There is no going back to Roanoke for Mama. "Thank you for caring for our Mama," I say. Perk and Teddy are already walking out the door to pull the car around.

The rain has let up by the time we park in front of Gentle Healing. There are no staff in sight. Perk gets out of the car with the paperwork in hand and Teddy and I watch her walk through the door. Ten minutes go by before we see her pushing a wheelchair towards us. I can see Perk's face tighten as she approaches.

"Those people were going to make us wait until the shift change at four." I told the girl at the desk, I said, "is my mother's room ready? Because we are paying for this entire day and it should be." Perk shakes her head back and forth. "It is three o-clock, what did they think we were going to do with her for an hour?"

"Well," Teddy sighs, "we are here now, let's get moving." He smiles at Perk and rubs her neck. "Calm down, Perk."

Perk looks at Teddy hard for a second or two and then opens the back door and smiles at Mama. "C'mon Mama, this is your home away from home for a few days."

Mama smiles, her eyes still vacant but searching. I take her hand and whisper, "Just for a little while, until you heal, Mama."

There is a heaviness to an old person when you are trying to lift them, almost a dead weight, and hoisting Mama from a seated position in a Ford Escape took some doing. First Teddy tries to lift the good arm and then Perk steps in and lifts her bottom and finally Mama is able to step up on the curb. I pull the wheelchair right up to her backside and Perk eases her down. The lobby is empty except for the woman Perk dealt with, and even though I smile at her she doesn't smile back. The smell of urine fills my nostrils and I try to breathe through my mouth.

Perk knows the room number and walks ahead of us. Teddy pushes Mama and tells her about the new business opportunity he read about on Facebook. A renowned orthopedist has produced a senior multi-vitamin that focuses on bone health and is selling them in bulk, wholesale. I follow behind and chew my cheek as I pass the residents bent down over their wheelchairs, lining the hallway, staring down at nothing at all. I want to turn around and push Mama right out of here. I want to take her home. I want Mama back. Perk marches on and I breathe a sigh of relief when we reach Mama's room. The other bed is empty, thank goodness for that.

Perk helps Mama from the wheelchair and into the bed. Teddy leaves and comes back a few minutes later with an aide. "Hello, Mrs. Smith, my name is Mary. Is there anything I can get you?"

Mama smiles and says nothing.

"Can you get her a glass of water and a blanket for the bed?" Perk is not smiling, but she does ask this lightly. "I am her daughter Perk, and this is my sister Pauline and my husband Teddy."

"Oh yes, I met Teddy, he tracked me down on my rounds and was very persuasive." Mary grins at Teddy and he grins back. Teddy could calm a rattler if needed. "It is very nice to meet you all. We will take good care of your mother."

I hang on to Mary's words as we leave Mama sipping her water through a straw, the blanket tucked around her body, and the television tuned to the Ellen Show.

"Well," I say as we drive away from Gentle Healing, "that place is awful. I don't want Mama there. Mary seems nice, but did you smell the urine?"

"She's not there forever, Pauline. But she can't go back to her apartment, we have to find her something more, assisted living, memory care, I don't know, but this is a necessary evil to get Mama better."

"I know," I say. "But I hate it." Every bit of gray sky has turned to blue and the sun is bright with the afternoon light even though it feels like it should be midnight. We drive the rest of the way to my house in silence. My heart aches for what is coming. I want to run back in time, shelter in my childhood before my daddy died, live again through those lazy summers, eat silver queen and butter beans, peach ice cream on the churn, and chase lightning bugs till the cowbell rings, calling Perk and I home for bedtime.

14

Moving On

PERK AND TEDDY DROP ME OFF at my house and wave as they pull away. Every nerve in my body is as tight as a tick. As I open the front door and walk inside, the space where the loafers stay is empty. I am too tired to look for them, but the sight of the empty space makes me smile. *Mama's caring for me still*, I think. I take a hot soaking bath and then put on my nightgown. The leftover Salisbury Steak Lean Cuisine in my refrigerator is not at all satisfying, but I sit and chew at my kitchen table in a kind of trance. My heart feels dull and far away and then hurts like I'm being stabbed. I am not ready for this change. I wash my plate and go back to the bedroom, soft tears streaming down my face.

I sleep long and deep. I don't think I turn over once, and when I wake the next morning I feel rested, hopeful. Even before I heat up the coffee, I lay down beside my bed and peek underneath. Mama's loafers sit glowing in the corner by the bedpost. I stand up and sigh, filling my lungs deep with sweet breath.

I fix myself a good breakfast of scrambled eggs and toast and admire my own cooking on the plate. Sometimes there is nothing more satisfying than cooking yourself a favorite meal and enjoying every bite even more because you made it for yourself. I sit at the kitchen table and chew. *Maybe Gentle Healing won't be as bad as I think.*

I finish eating and wash the dishes before calling Perk. "I'm going to visit Mama this morning." I expect Perk to try to talk me out of it, tell me Mama is fine and taken care of.

"Good," she says, "I'll go this afternoon. Until we see how things are there, we'll both go, double duty." I hang up and feel my worry return. When Perk says double duty I can be sure she thinks something needs doing. I sigh as I get dressed, my stomach already beginning to churn.

By the time I arrive at Gentle Healing the night shift has left and the day shift of nurses and aides are hustling up and down the hallway. You would think they were all late to catch a bus, barely giving anyone eye contact. To be fair, I don't think there are enough of them to do their jobs right even if they want to, and from the looks of them they don't enjoy being here at all. I have met toll booth attendants who enjoy their jobs more. I look at each one of them, hoping to see Mary or any friendly face. The only person who smiles at me is an old woman bent over her wheelchair, calling out to me, "Denise, Denise, so good to see you."

I smile back and keep walking. The urine smell is even stronger this morning. Mama is awake when I walk in her room, sitting up, staring out her one window that looks out to a little courtyard of benches and geranium-filled barrels.

"Hey Mama."

She looks over at me and I see the dullness in her eyes. "Get me to the bathroom, Pauline."

There is a stain near the middle of her bedsheet. The covers are down around her ankles and her nightgown is open at the bottom, the snaps undone. I can see the same diaper the hospital put on Mama yesterday sagging. I am so mad I can spit nails. I am ready to go find whoever I can and yell at them for not changing my mother's diaper, for not even taking her to the bathroom.

Mama watches me, then looks down and says, "Pauline, there comes a time when things that used to matter just don't." She says this with such a tiredness that it practically breaks my heart. This is the saddest thing I have ever heard Mama say.

I help her out of bed and hold her steady as she uses the walker to get to the bathroom. It is a slow process, and we are not even halfway to the bathroom when an aide walks in. "Can you please help us?" Mama and I both stare at her. For one second I am not sure she will, but she comes over and adjusts the walker and helps Mama the rest of the way to the bathroom and onto the toilet.

As the aide is removing the diaper, I say from the doorway, "Someone needs to come in here and check on Mama and see if she needs to go to the bathroom. That diaper came with her from the hospital." I use my stern voice but she barely nods. "And please change the sheets. Now."

Margo, her name tag says, looks at me briefly and then leaves. I am about to chase her down the hall and then remember Mama. Once she is finished using the bathroom, I take the new diaper and help her step into it. Mama is weak as a kitten and doesn't fuss at all as I struggle to lift her bottom and pull her back onto the wheelchair. As I am rolling her out to the hall Margo comes back, sheets in hand. I thank her as I push Mama away.

I spend the next hour pushing her down the hallways and eventually out onto the courtyard. The air still holds the morning dew and the shade from the nearby maple trees shade us from the sun. As I sit on a bench beside her, I breathe in the moment. Mama sits quiet.

"Nice morning" she finally says.

We both smile. "Nice morning," I say.

When I call Perk later to tell her what happened, she practically barks into the phone. "Those people don't even change her diaper? I don't care if Medicare is footing the bill, we are paying for better service than this. I'll talk to the manager this afternoon." Perk sighs. "And I don't care how long they want to keep her, no matter how long Medicare approves her, we are finding her another place, Pauline. It might take us awhile, but we are getting her out of there."

We hang up and the hopefulness of our conversation stays with me most of the day.

It turns out Perk is right to say moving Mama is going to take a while. Everyone she talks to at other rehabilitation centers tells her the same thing. *No beds.* And when I look up the ratings for Gentle Healing on the internet, it gets four out of five stars. Days turn into weeks and with each day Mama fades from us a little more. Her eyes remain dull even when we visit, her body shrinks, and her appetite for anything but a few sips of dark chocolate Ensure drops to nothing at all.

My days follow the same routine, visiting Mama at Gentle Healing, complaining to the staff about her care, and bringing Mama chocolate bars and cinnamon buns to try to stir her appetite. There is one silver lining about management by crisis you can count on. All of a sudden time before the crisis blurs, losing importance and even presence. I haven't thought about Bob or his crazy wife much since Mama fell. The days and nights are only about the immediate, feeding the cats, fitting in the time to take a bath and get a little sleep and grocery shop before heading back to the nursing home. And if I happen to arrive at the nursing home at the times the shifts are changing, I can forget about any kind of update on

Mama. The information I might need from the night shift is already walking out the door.

Mama has been in the nursing home for a month when Perk and Teddy invite me over for dinner. Teddy has made his famous chili, which is mostly hamburger meat, beer, and hot peppers, and I can picture Perk in the kitchen, setting out a bowl of chips and grated cheese to go along with it. When I get there I use my key at the door to let myself in. Before I'm even through the door the bird flies past me and up the stairs to the second floor. Perk has moved his cage to the guest bedroom after Teddy complained that he couldn't eat dinner in peace with the bird chirping and eyeing his plate. The guest bedroom looks out on the backyard oak tree full of robins and sparrows and wrens. That bird has free reign to peck on the windowsill and chirp along with all the birds outside. Ever since he got his own bedroom he flies up there whenever anyone comes over, and then announces himself from the second floor for so long Teddy ends up closing the bedroom door, leaving a muffled chirping as background noise the entire time you are visiting. You would think they had a teenager living up there, for all the commotion it causes.

While we are eating dinner, Perk lays out a plan. "I wouldn't say this to anyone but you and Teddy, Pauline, but it would have been better for Mama if she had just fallen over and died."

My eyes water as quick as a downpour, and I blurt out, "Perk!"

"Oh you know what I mean, Pauline. Mama's lived her life strong, independent and as sharp-minded as a tack. We both know she realizes, even if only part of the time, that her mind is going, that she is slipping away. She wouldn't want any of this. She would want to live on Yellow Mountain in the house she and Daddy bought, and she would want to die there. All this, as much as she loves us, she just wouldn't want, Pauline."

Perk's eyes are watering too, and she quickly wipes them and looks about as sad as I have seen her since Daddy died. I cringe as I think about Mama living out the remaining days of her life at Gentle Healing, or at any nursing home. In the days after Mama fell, Perk and I called up a half dozen nursing homes, went to visit two of them, and discovered we either couldn't afford them or else couldn't bear the thought of Mama ending up there. The options were all overwhelming and downright depressing.

I nod, even though the thought was not an easy one for me. There is so much time between being a child and being an older adult where every step of the way you have had your mother by your side, that it just doesn't leave room for understanding your life without her. The thought of Mama gone is unnatural, and when I say this to Perk, she shakes her head.

"Pauline, Mama wouldn't want to keep going if she couldn't stand on her own. Do you think Mama in her right mind would ever say something like 'some things don't matter'? Hard as this sounds, truth is truth."

I stare at Perk and nod, but inside a quiet panic is taking hold, and the fear of losing Mama grips me.

Teddy speaks up then, saying, "Now hold on. I have some news and you both need to hear this." Teddy's eyes light up like he has just found the prize in the Cracker Jack box.

"Oh good lord," Perk says now, breaking the grip my panic holds on me.

"Not now, Teddy," I say, looking over at Perk. This is just not the time to hear about another investment scheme.

"This is about your Mama."

"What about Mama?" Perk snaps.

Teddy smiles like he is sitting on the prize. "Do you all remember when we used to have those Super Bowl parties, back when I was still working at the bank?"

I did. Teddy would make his chili and line up bowls of chips and salsa and cornbread on the counter and stand at the stove scooping out chili to anyone who walked through the door. It was the one time of the year when he took over the kitchen and held his court.

"Gary came every year."

"Oh sure, tall wavy-haired fellow, always asking for your chili recipe?" Perk asks.

"That's Gary. We worked together until I retired, and he would have stayed there until he retired too if he hadn't been injured. He fell off a ladder cleaning the gutters last fall and was paralyzed head to toe."

"So sad," Perk says, shaking her head.

I nod, even though I only met Gary once several years ago at the Super Bowl party.

"Well, his wife Sharon still lives in their house, but Gary has been in a nursing home ever since the accident." Teddy is becoming more animated. "I was at Kroger's, standing in line at the checkout, and Sharon walked up. We got to talking and I asked about Gary and she said he was about the same and the line was long so I told her about your Mama falling and how you and Perk were looking to move her. Sharon asked if I'd ever heard of a place called Coming Home. Have you?"

"No." Perk and I both say at the same time.

"Well," Teddy goes on, "Sharon's cousin's mother-in-law, who is almost as old as your Mama and suffers dementia, couldn't live on her own anymore, and Sharon's cousin moved her there. Sharon says she loves it. It is half as expensive as an assisted living or nursing home would be." Teddy's eyes are gleaming now. "And, it is just a house, a big house, where the aides serve home-cooked meals and the churches come out to visit every week. They only take ten people, so I guess the only way they have openings is when someone dies, but Sharon said her cousin's mother-in-law went there without even having to get on a waiting list."

I am looking at Teddy and then at Perk and trying to follow, but the only piece of the news that sinks in is that Mama really will have to move. Again. We both had hoped Mama's last days would be at her apartment, surrounded by her memories and our portraits and the antique furniture she cherished, but we both know now that is not going to happen. In the time since the fall, Mama's body has begun to shut down and her mind stays mostly in a fog.

Perk is smiling and nodding her head up and down. "Oh good lord Teddy, you have been sitting on this news all day?"

"I wanted you both to hear it at the same time." Teddy grins and keeps grinning until both Perk and I start grinning too.

"It does sound promising, doesn't it, Pauline?" Perk is looking at me, waiting for me to agree.

I nod yes. I know in my heart, it is time. Mama is ready.

"You know Pauline," Perk says now, "I think the least we can do is go out and visit this place."

My feet start to tap under the table, the feelings rolling through me, excitement that we might just have a place for Mama, fear that this is getting too close to the end. "Okay," I say.

Driving home, I start making a to-do list in my mind of Mama things – what clothes to pick up at her apartment at Serenity, which paintings to take when we move her to Coming Home. We had kept the apartment while Mama was in the nursing home, waiting to see if she would get strong enough to return to her apartment. Perk had called Laura last week and cancelled the lease. Fortunately, it was a month to month lease, and we could get the furniture moved before it ended. All of this is swirling around and around in my head with such a fever I am feeling a little dizzy as I pull into the driveway. Walking into the house, I barely notice the envelope on the floor by the mail slot. I give both Jimbo and Sassy a head rub and walk to the kitchen to feed them their Fancy Feast. It's almost an afterthought taking the envelope with me. I open it at the kitchen table while I fix myself a baking soda and water to drink. Teddy's chili is a favorite of mine, but take the stress I'm feeling over Mama, and it's no mystery why my stomach tends to act up. Granddaddy used to say the best neutralizer for an angry stomach was the alkaline. He always kept the baking soda box with a little spoon and glass inside his medicine cabinet.

Inside the envelope there is a note with a picture of a red robin sitting on a branch, and handwritten on the inside.

> Dear Pauline,
> Sally told me about calling you. She didn't tell me until today or else I would have come by sooner. I am sorry. Can we talk? My number is on the back of the card.
> Yours,
> Bob.

Looking at the note, all I can think is, *Who even does that, sends a bird note as an apology?* The pain in my heart for Bob feels small and hard. Reggie had been a liar, and I see now Bob is too. That night after Sally Redford called, sitting at the kitchen table sipping brandy, I felt like all my feelings for Bob had to be packed up and tossed aside like a box for the donation bin. A broken trust is no trust at all, and a heart can't fill without trust. As I sat there, I said a silent thanks that Sally Redford had called me and shed the light. I'll be honest, I was cussing her and Bob as much as I was hurting. The pain I was feeling was just not as strong as the injustice I felt.

I throw the envelope and the note into the trash and bundle up the bag to walk it out to the super can. Outside, the sky is full of stars sprinkled around a half moon, and even though the night is not much cooler than the day that's gone, the air holds a freshness to it. There is nothing but quiet, even though this is the time of night the neighborhood dogs have been let out to entertain themselves. The time when they mostly bark. Tonight, though, there is nothing but quiet.

15

Coming Home

MAMA TURNS 97 IN THE NURSING HOME. The weeks in the nursing home have grown into a month and counting, and there is not a sign of brightness about her even when I bring her chocolate. If there was ever a reason to move her out of that place, turning her nose up at chocolate is a sure sign.

Perk and Teddy and I went to visit the Coming Home Senior Home and lined up a room for Mama. They had two beds from the recent deaths of a woman who was 99 and one who had just turned 84. During our visit, we passed hospice nurses and pastors in the hallway, and everyone there was smiling as we passed them. Everyone has their own financial situation to consider, but the one thing no one is going to promote is the fact that the services the hospitals and some of the nursing homes provide, even though those services might be covered by Medicare, are not necessarily a good thing or a loving thing. Coming Home Senior Home was both good and loving, as well as inexpensive.

Before we move Mama, the nurse supervisor tells Perk and me a good ten times, "BUT it is covered by Medicare. Your mother can stay with us another month."

There is not a reason in the world to try to explain to that woman that, no matter how much money it is going to cost us, we're not going to smother the last bit of joy in our mother's life by letting her stay in a place like that. They've done their best, but that best isn't even close to good.

By the time we get Mama moved in and settled at Coming Home, Perk and I are convinced that any place but the nursing home would be fine. Mama lost weight she couldn't afford to lose at the nursing home and looks to have shrunk down to a shell. I haven't seen a smile on her face or a twinkle in her eyes since before she was in the hospital. The day we move Mama is hot as fire by 10AM. Teddy pushes her wheelchair up the long wooden ramp that leads to the rancher's front door. From the road, you would think Coming Home is just a family's wide brick house like anybody else's, with a covered patio on one side and a glassed-in sunroom on the other. Perk rings the buzzer and a short black woman answers the door, smiling ear to ear.

"Good morning," she says in an accent that lilts and twirls like a song, "You must be Eloise." She leans down and takes Mama's hand. "I am Serena and we are going to become very good friends."

Mama looks up at Serena and holds her gaze, even though her eyes remain dull and vacant.

"And you are Eloise's daughters?"

I am impressed right away that this woman knows who we are and seems downright happy to see us. Serena shows us into the living room where the residents sit in wheelchairs facing a television. Eight old ladies look over at us and the two sitting at the back smile and wave. Another woman sits off to the side holding a baby doll, and in the seat beside her, another baby doll lays across the seat. Serena waves to them all and steers us to the back of the house, to Mama's room. A large bay window looks out onto a green field on the other side of Mama's bed. She will be able to see such a pretty view. I swallow hard to keep tears from welling.

"This is lovely," Perk says. "Should I put Mama's clothes in the closet, Serena? We brought the diapers too."

"Oh I can do that. Eloise is in good hands." Serena smiles at each of us and then adds, "Eloise and I are going to use the walker and visit the bathroom soon." She points to a walker in the closet. "A warm sponge bath and fresh clothes always bring the smiles back. Go on, we are fine. Come back to visit tomorrow. I will make sure Eloise settles in."

I let out a sigh that sounds like I have been holding my breath too long and Serena looks over at me and laughs. "Here we love our residents. We are family, Pauline. You do not need to worry."

"Thank you so much," Perk says, "we have been so worried." She lets out a sigh and reaches her arms out, hugging Serena. "This is so comforting."

"We will take good care of Eloise." Serena says, still smiling.

"Serena, what time tomorrow can I come visit?" I say.

"The church ladies come in the morning to sing. Come for lunch, Pauline."

I wasn't certain I wanted to sit down with all those old folks for lunch, and my face must have showed that.

"Pauline," Serena says, her blue eyes sparkling, "the only way you will relax and see how Eloise is loved here is to share this time with us. You and Eloise are both at home here." She looks over to Teddy and Perk and adds, "And Teddy and Perk, you are too."

"Serena," Perk says, "I am trying to put a finger on your accent and I just cannot. Where are you from?"

Serena laughs and says, "Liberia." she says it almost like a three-word sentence in case we cannot understand exactly what she is saying. "Li-ber-ia. In A-fri-ca."

Serena is still smiling as we each lean down and kiss Mama good-bye.

"I'll see you tomorrow for lunch, Mama. Thank you, Serena," I say. As we walk out past the living room, the same two women at the back wave to us. Teddy, Perk, and I all wave back.

Perk is driving away from Coming Home when she says, "Well, I've never met anyone else from Liberia, but Serena is sure sweet. Where is Liberia, anyway?"

"She told us, Africa," Teddy says, pulling out his phone and typing something on the screen. "It is a country in West Africa. The oldest one to declare itself a republic."

"That is something," Perk says. "I think Mama is in a good place now."

"I do too," I say.

The air conditioning in the car is turned up to max as Perk drives, the three of us quiet. I can hear my neck muscles crunching as I move my head from side to side. As they drop me off at my house, I smile. *Mama's in a good place now*, I think.

The next day, I stop by Kroger's and buy a chocolate sheet cake with chocolate icing and drive over to Coming Home. It is Mama's favorite cake and I want to bring something as a thank you to Serena and the rest of the staff. I am walking toward the bakery counter when Jeremy appears at the end of the dog food aisle.

"Hey, Pauline."

I can feel my face heating up as I take a deep breath and say, "Hey, Jeremy."

"How's your Mama? I heard you moved her."

"We did. After she fell, she just couldn't get around like she needs to on her own." Sweat is trickling down my neck. Jeremy is looking at me like he sees a prize, and it sends desire stirring through me. As much as I distrust all men except Teddy at this moment, I can't stop the stirring.

"I miss seeing your sweet Mama, Pauline. And it sure is nice seeing you. We should do this more often." Jeremy winks at me, grins, and says, "Well I have to get to work. Bye now," as he walks away.

I am undone. The man doesn't know me. He's got no business flirting. "Bye," I say, flushed, my heart beating fast. I hurry over to the bakery counter and pick out a sheet cake. There is just something about that Jeremy that makes me feel like I am sixteen again. As I leave, I look around for him, but he is nowhere in sight.

I have finally started breathing normal when I drive up to Coming Home. Balancing the cake with one hand, I ring the buzzer. Serena answers.

"Pauline, what have you brought here?" Serena is smiling as I step through the door.

"A cake. I want to say thank you for welcoming Mama." I smile, my eyes beginning to water. The sharp contrast between the Gentle Healing nursing home and Coming Home brings on these grateful tears.

Serena gently lifts the cake from my hands and carries it back to the kitchen. I glance over at the dining room and see all the old ladies seated around the long wooden table. Mama is on the far side, seated next to the woman with the baby dolls. The woman is small and bent over her plate, her white hair thin and barely covering her skull, and she holds a baby doll in her lap. Next to her, there is a booster chair, with another baby doll folded over the seat, and a little plate of applesauce on the tray. Mama is eating a piece of fried chicken with her fingers. The sight of Mama eating anything at all drops my jaw. Her plate is full of small dollops—creamed corn, lima beans, applesauce—foods Mama grew up with.

I walk over and sit down next to her, kiss her forehead, and say, "Hey Mama."

She looks up and smiles. "Hey Pauline. Go fix yourself a plate."

Serena comes back out of the kitchen then with a plate piled high and sets it in front of me. "You and Eloise can both use some meat on your bones."

"How did you get Mama to eat, she wasn't eating at all at that nursing home?" I am smiling, but the shock I feel is bound to show.

"Your Mama knows she is loved here. And food cooked with love is always delicious." Serena looks around the table and says, "See, we all eat together and eat well here. Food is good."

I look around the table and see all of the women bent over their plates, spooning up food. Some of the women are in a trance staring vacantly over their plates, but the two women on the end are chatting about something that has them laughing and nodding their heads up and down. I recognize them as the two who waved at us yesterday. *Well, I think, at least there are two people here lucid enough to talk.* I spoon up a bite of the creamed corn and taste the butter and salt and cream, a delight on my tongue. Home cooking. I feel a warmth filling me and I do not know if it is the delicious food or the twinkle in Serena's eyes or just the sight of Mama eating, but my heart is comforted. I can get used to visits like this.

Mama's been at Coming Home for several weeks when Serena calls me at home. She wants to know if I can buy Mama new underwear and pants in a larger size. And a pair of tennis shoes a size larger because Mama's feet are swelling. I am immediately worried about the swelling, but I'm too relaxed to worry very long. After all, Mama is walking on her own again.

"Your Mama," Serena says, "has started getting up before the others and walking into the kitchen to make herself a cup of coffee." As soon as Serena says this I prepare myself, thinking it will be a repeat of Laura at Serenity calling to complain about Mama, but Serena just keeps on talking and laughing with a lightness about her that makes me want to drop my shoulders and laugh right along with her.

"Pauline, you will need to bring her also the slippers with rubber soles too, so that she doesn't slip. We are trying to encourage her to stay in bed until we come to get her in the morning." Serena starts laughing again. "She tells us if we aren't going to come get her earlier she will just meet us in the kitchen. Your mother has also told me she would like to do the grocery shopping. She would like cinnamon buns. She is stronger by the day, Pauline."

Serena's words were pure music to my ears, and they fill me with a joy so full of relief from the stress of Mama's fall and hardships of the months since, a release so freeing I practically jump up and down while she is talking. There are times when hearing about the simplest progress can mean the most.

I can't say there has ever been a Target shopping day I have not enjoyed, but today, shopping for Mama, I am having one of my most entertaining Target shopping days ever. I even take the time to look over the new bedding displays, before strolling through the Target flash sale aisles, the ones where every item has been marked down to practically nothing and the prices are circled with that bold red Target emblem. To say I am feeling festive would be exactly right.

I drive home singing to the radio, belting out along with Tom Petty, "*The waiting is the hardest part*", feeling as light as air as I pull up to the house. A strange Ford pick-up is parked in front of my house, and when I park the car I see Bob stooped down to my mail slot. There are some days so bright not one thing can shadow them, and this is one of them. I still feel my heart clutch and my teeth tighten, but seeing him here feels so out of place. He is a stranger. A lifetime has passed since his crazy wife called me, since I felt like Bob was here to stay. Walking up to the door, I say, "Bob, what are you doing here?" My tone is not a bit friendly.

He is still bent over, staring up at me, his face scruffy and looking like he has seen the last of a good razor. Rising up, he tips his ball cap down and says, "Pauline, I need to explain." He holds up another envelope.

I can already guess there is another bird card inside, and without even stopping myself, I blurt out, "Mama fell. Not long after that crazy wife of yours called me, Bob. Go home to your wife." I shift my hips back a bit and continue, "I don't have any time for your nonsense. And stop bringing those cards here. They are just littering my doorway."

"Pauline," Bob says, "I am real sorry about your Mama. I hope she gets better soon. Please let me just explain. Sally is on medication, and when she doesn't take it she gets real paranoid." Bob looks at me as if what he has just said will make all the difference in the world. "I did tell Sally about our friendship, how I had finally found another person in this town to talk to, really talk to."

I am staring at Bob and thinking how very little he has ever said about himself and realize he is as delusional as she is. I start taking measured breaths. I am not alarmed, just very set on getting inside my house. I inch myself past him.

"But then she got in one of her fits and I found out later, she had stopped her medication again and then she told me she had talked to you. It's my fault for mentioning your last name. She knew my mail route so it was easy for her to look up your number. I am so sorry, Pauline."

I am watching Bob and listening to him talk, and all I can think about is how he is a stranger to me now and for some reason he reminds me of Myra. When Perk and I were kids, Granny always had Sunday lunch after church, when the cousins and Aunt Eleanor and Uncle Bart and Aunt Florence and Mama and Perk and me and Daddy would sit around a long dining room table crammed with straight-backed cane chairs to fit everyone in. After we had all sat down and the table had been filled with vegetables and meats and fruits and breads, there would come Myra, Granny's friend from church who was older than Mama and Aunt Eleanor and Aunt Florence, and younger than Granny.

Myra was always late because she sang in the choir, and Granny always made her welcome and found a chair to fit her in at the table, usually a corner where she had to lean real far forward to reach her plate. And even though Myra smiled and listened to all the chatter and yelling all of us might do, she always seemed apart. Not a part of our family, but even more than that, apart from everywhere, like she was floating somewhere above us and we were all holding on to her with a string. I remember Myra as that, and as the gray lady. Gray hair, skin a dusty gray, and a voice so soft it floated over you like a cloud, a gray cloud.

That is what strikes me today about Bob. He is not all here, apart from everywhere, and becoming grayer in his look and his manner. I have yet to think anyone can ruin another; like Mama always said, you make your own choices, and Bob made his when he married Sally. I don't know this man, and realize I don't want to.

"Bob, why in the world did you tell me you were divorced and hide your wedding ring?"

"I don't know. Sally and I have been going through a hard time. I didn't want to think about her while I was out here working."

"But you lied, Bob. And I can't be friends with a liar. And you are still not wearing your wedding ring."

"Oh, that's just habit. I never wore it working. See, here it is, I keep it in my pocket."

I shake my head. When I look at him, all I see is the lie. Reggie would do the same thing. Explain away a lie he was telling me, make it sound like it was the most reasonable thing in the world. Bob may not be selling prescription painkillers, but he is a married man lying about it. I cannot think of another thing left to say to Bob, other than what I do say. "I hope you and Sally can get through this, Bob. I truly do, but to be perfectly honest I don't have one minute of time to listen to anything else you have to say."

I walk into the house and close the door behind me, slip off my loafers and leave them beside the door, but not before I give them an extra pat, for protection, or encouragement, or maybe just for the love of them and all they represent. Tiredness washes over me. It has been a day. I walk back into my bedroom and turn on the heated mattress pad and television. Another rerun of Law and Order is on, and I settle in without even a thought of brushing my teeth. I stare at the screen and listen to Olivia Benson interviewing a victim, and let my mind empty.

As I am drifting off to sleep, I see a peculiar thing. I am standing in the middle of a rushing river, standing in water up to my knees, peaceful, watching time rush by and stand still at the same time. I can't put my finger on the why of it, but I cannot say it is an unsettling feeling, just peculiar.

I am usually very good at turning off the television and all the lights before I go to sleep. Energy costs money, and if there is one thing anybody can do to pinch pennies it is to cut off lights. I am faithful to that usually, but for whatever reason I fall asleep with all of the lights turned on, the house as bright as a day and the television running right along like it is a regular evening. And I sleep as soundly as I can remember, and dream the silliest dream of standing on a boogie board, like the rounded little curved board I took to Virginia Beach when I was a child, the one I would throw out into the surf and race behind, barely hopping on top of it to win my ride across a wave, more times than not missing the board entirely. In my dream I am standing on this boogie board, skimming the top of an ending wave along a beach, with no clothes on and a floppy hat and not a care in the world, no one in sight and the feeling of gliding, skimming the surface of the shallow wave, as light as a puff of air.

I wake up early, before the sun is anywhere close to rising, and wake up smiling. I lie still, remembering the dream. The television morning show is on, and I reach over for the remote and turn it off. There is a deepness to this silent house, like a mountain after newly fallen snow. Just as I am about to get out of bed, the phone rings. Nothing good happens when a phone rings early, and sure enough, when I answer I hear

Perk, her voice low and steady, the tone she uses when there is a largeness to what she has to say.

"Pauline," she says now, "Mama died. We're coming over now to get you."

"What?" I say, unsure I've heard right.

Perk lets out a deep sigh. "Serena went to check on her at midnight and she was fine, sleeping soundly, and again at three, and then when she came back this morning, Mama was gone."

I am thinking of the pants I just bought Mama at Target, the smile she gave me when I was leaving yesterday, and I cannot for the life of me register that she is gone. The cold is spreading through me.

"Pauline," Perk says now, her voice breaking softly, then steady "you know Mama, she is going to leave when she is good and ready. I think her old body was just waiting until she was comfortable."

We hang up and I walk over to the dresser, wondering for a half a second if I have any clean underwear. I dress and walk out to the hallway to slip on my loafers. I get right up to the door and see they are gone. Without a thought, I walk in a trance back to the bedroom. Mama died. I roll this over my mind again and again as I lay down with my cheek pressed into the scatter rug and stare, eyes widening even as tears begin to spill, first slowly, then all of a sudden in heaves and shudders. Light hasn't yet come through the window, but underneath my bed, surrounding those loafers, I sense the light glowing yellow and white with flecks of gold. And in spite of my pain, the light washes over me and surrounds me and I feel Mama holding me, whispering, "You are going to be alright."

I reach in and gently touch the soft leather of the loafers. In that moment I felt the glowing inside of me, warming me.

In that moment, Mama's presence surrounds me, surrounds those loafers, and I know that it's been Mama all along, here with me, moving those loafers, maybe just to get my attention or to tell me to pay attention. It doesn't matter. What matters is Mama is here, with me. I believe that and so it is true for me.

I slip the loafers on and walk out to meet Perk and Teddy. They are both walking toward me, arms outstretched, and for a few minutes in the early morning light we stand together outside of the car and cry, and hold each other, and don't say a word. The three of us drive over to Coming Home, the quiet surrounding us like a hug, hushed and warm.

There are times when you question a person's death, the why and the how of it. With Mama, at 97, it wasn't a matter of questioning. We knew she had lived long enough, and the how and the why of it didn't much matter. Besides, knowing Mama like we did, it made perfect sense that she would be the one to decide when she left.

The three of us arrive at Coming Home as the residents are getting up from breakfast, the woman with the baby dolls is being helped to rise by one aide while another picks up the babies and follows to her room. Serena leads us back to Mama's room, Perk stepping forward with a surety of purpose, me with the hesitating step of someone scared of ghosts, and Teddy behind the both of us, holding up the rear. Mama is there, lying on her bed, still wearing her Mama smile, and I see a light still in her eyes as she gazes up at our portraits on the wall beside her. The aides have cleaned and dressed her in a fresh nightgown, and left her lying in the bed as peaceful as a prayer. I don't know if it is her smile alone or the look of love in her eyes, but I know right then Mama approves, she is at peace and happy. She is going home.

"Serena, her eyes look so beautiful."

"Your Mama died with love in her eyes," Serena says softly. "We haven't closed them yet. We wanted you to see her love even in death."

I suppose Serena has watched over families saying their good-byes many times while working at Coming Home, but she cares for us now like we are her own, holding me while I cry and listening to Perk as she thanks her over and over for her kindness and care for Mama. The four of us stand beside Mama's bed, huddled together, talking softly, for what is awhile. I look down and feel my roots right there in those loafers, holding me upright, holding me.

For the life of me I couldn't have imagined the hours next would be spent sitting in the Coming Home dining room waiting for someone from the medical examiner's office to inspect the body. In spite of Mama's easy passing, the brand new medical examiner on-call is not of the mind to let Mama go anywhere until someone from his office can come out and investigate and what all else they need to do. So, we sit there, with Serena and the sheriff, making small talk.

The sheriff's name is Sam Brady and he is somewhere between my age and Perk's. Old enough to be retired, barrel chested and with a laugh as big as a rodeo call. Sam has been called in because that's what happens when you don't die in a hospital. The state needs to make sure you haven't been murdered. Sam takes one look at us and apologizes for the wait.

"I am so sorry for your loss. I'll make this as quick as I can so you folks can get home."

He takes his pad and pencil out and starts asking us questions about Mama, how often we visited, how she had fallen, why we had moved her here. He is respectful with those questions, and before long Perk and I are telling him stories about Mama. Sam puts his pencil down and listens, bursting out with that belly laugh when we tell him about Mama calling every one of us constitutional inadequates and how she would climb the fire stairs at the Serenity every day.

The afternoon passes and Sam calls that medical examiner twice asking where the person was and could he let us all please go home. After he hangs up the phone the second time, Sam looks at us and says, "That medical examiner is too young and green to know sense from fiction."

We all shake our heads and Perk says, "It's a good thing Mama's dead, else she would already be out here and driving herself to that morgue."

"I already feel like I know your Mama," Sam says, smiling.

We sit quiet for a while longer, until we all hear the tires crunching on the driveway outside and see the long black hearse winding towards us out the window.

I'm not sure who sighs loudest, but I suspect it is Sam.

16

Carrying On

NOBODY TALKS TO YOU ABOUT THE BUSINESS OF DEATH, all the irritations that come with finalizing a person's life and sending them off. The condolences come and every one of them has to do with missing the person, grieving the person, honoring the person. And that is all fine, but it is hard to focus on grieving and honoring when you are still arguing with a medical examiner about releasing your dead Mama's body.

Since Mama was not under a doctor's care in the days leading up to the fall, her death is being investigated as suspicious. Perk calls a few days after Mama died to tell me.

"Suspicious," Perk says, sounding like her last nerve has been plucked. "I told the woman who answered the phone, I said, 'does the medical examiner even know how old she was?' The poor woman was just a secretary, but I could not hold my tongue. I asked her point blank, I said, 'is it our fault our Mama didn't need a doctor, wasn't complaining of a thing, other than falling down?' It is enough to make you wonder why those people get paid, and it is our hard-earned tax money paying them. An autopsy for a woman 97 years old, fine, but how long can that take? Every one of her organs must have been on their last breath. It will be a wonder if there is anything left for him to even poke and prod."

The days after Mama died go by just as sudden and slow as the ones right after she fell. Full of waiting on the medical examiner and letting the world know she is gone. I suppose it was good timing that we had already packed up most of Mama's things when we moved her out of the apartment and over to Coming Home. I don't even fill the back seat with what is left at Coming Home, but it is good to go back and hug Serena and the other women one more time. I give the lady with the baby dolls a wave and pat the dolls' heads, and even though she doesn't smile, her eyes come into focus for just a moment.

Three more bird cards come during those days after Mama died. A blue jay, a wren, and a chickadee, all with little notes from Bob, mostly saying, *Sorry*. My blood boils just a little when I open them, pouring salt in the wound, reminding me what a fool I've been, calling up a pang of loneliness. Forgiving myself is going to take a while.

Between the wait for the medical examiner to release the body and the cards littering the floor every time I come home, my nerves stretch as tight as a rubber band ready to shoot. The relatives have started calling, asking when we are holding the service. Our cousin Henry from Danville has called twice, but I haven't answered or called him back.

Ten days after Mama's death, with no word still from the medical examiner, I call Perk.

"Perk," I say, "the relatives are calling. What are we going to do?"

She just laughs her Perk laugh. "Pauline, your ears must have been burning. I called that medical examiner back this morning and spoke to him in person. I said, what is taking so long? Is she still alive? Because after ten days she either needs to be walking out of there or picked up by the funeral home. This is negligence."

"I didn't correct him one bit, but the man stuttered. I don't know if I made him nervous or if that was his affliction, but it took him a little while to get it out. But he did, finally, tell me the findings were end stage heart failure, kidney failure, and stage four diabetes. A laundry list, Pauline, and honestly, all I could think was, well of course, when Mama is ready to go, she turns out all the lights."

"When is he releasing her?" I say.

"Today," Perk tells me, "and he said he would call the funeral home to come get her. I told him I was calling the funeral home the second we hung up and told him I would be there in person to pick up the death certificate. I don't even know where his office is, but I am sure going to find it on my own. I wasn't about to ask that man for one thing."

I would have guessed that holding the body for ten days would be the biggest part of the business, but I would have been wrong. Arranging for the body is just the beginning, and we are not starting out easy. After Mama finally made it to the funeral home, Perk found out that the orders she had signed for cremation had been lost. The man who called up Perk the next day had asked for instructions on a coffin, and for the full payment.

When Perk tells me all this over the phone, she is still mad, and so I can only imagine what the man had heard in her voice when she told him. "If our mother is not cremated in the next twenty-four hours I am calling the health department, do you understand me? I gave you a check for the cremation a week ago and I have a signed copy of the document requesting cremation."

"Pauline," Perk says then, "I had to drive over to that funeral home with the document, and then write another check. I told him the stop payment I was going to need to put on the last check was a twenty-five-dollar fee and that I was deducting it from the cost of the cremation. He did not argue. Honestly, Mama has been more difficult dead than she ever was living, and this is not even her fault."

We both decide right then any service for Mama will have to wait a few months. The thought of cramming in a service and inviting all the relatives is more than either of us want to face. It is enough to get Mama settled in the cloisonne jar she bought on her honeymoon in San Francisco and put her in Perk's jelly cabinet. There is still the will to file in probate, too, even though Mama had already given Perk and me everything but what she needed to live on. The will is just the paperwork at the end, not the big surprise or big disappointment it is for some folks.

As Perk and I talk over our plan, I can hear Teddy in the background. We decide to finish up the year, go through the holidays, and in the spring, when the mountains are turning green, take Mama back to Roanoke to rest beside Daddy's plot at Evergreen Cemetery.

I hear Teddy calling out, "Perk, tell her about the trip."

"Oh right, Pauline," Perk says, "you and Teddy and I are going on a trip. You do not get to refuse, this was Mama's idea ten years ago. When she made me her power of attorney, she set up a bank account for just you and me, and I had to promise. We are going to Mama's favorite place, Pauline..."

We both say together, "San Francisco," and laugh.

"When?" I say. I am too floored to argue and too surprised that Mama was scheming with Perk ten years ago. Except that Mama always did look out for Perk and me, and from the looks of it, she's still doing that even now that she's dead. My mind spins with questions.

Teddy is laughing. "Pauline," Perk says, "you know Teddy, he was on his computer the day after Mama died, looking up flights and hotels. He's got the whole week laid out for us, Pauline. Remember that New Year's Eve after you and I had gone to bed, and Teddy sat up with Mama finishing two bottles of champagne? She told him every place she and Daddy had gone on their honeymoon. We are going for drinks at the Top of the Mark, and we'll stay at a fancy hotel and walk the same streets she and Daddy walked. We'll ride the streetcars and watch the fog rolling in. We have reservations at a restaurant over by the bay just for that, and close to the little boutique hotel we will be staying at that night, just so we can all drink and eat and walk back to the hotel without calling a cab. We are leaving in three weeks, and Pauline, we are going to live it up, Mama style."

I laugh. There will be times to cry and times to be serious with the memories of missing Mama, but right now she is here with us, taking us forward, reminding us all to live it up. And my guess is that will always be the way.

"Perk," I say, almost as an afterthought, "what's the name of the hotel by the bay?"

She laughs. "I don't know how he found it, but Teddy says it gets five stars on Travelocity. We are staying at The Boogie Boutique Village."

17

Friendly Skies

NEITHER PERK OR TEDDY IS GOOD AT HOLDING SECRETS, but neither one of them let on we were flying first class until we are standing in the security line at the Richmond Airport and Teddy is passing me my ticket.

"Your mama was bossy about it, Pauline, like she always was, insisted we travel first class." Teddy starts laughing then and I think I have never loved him more than seeing that joy in his eyes as he remembers his talk with Mama. I am already nervous about flying. My last flight was down to Fort Lauderdale with Reggie so many years ago all the airlines have since changed their names.

I have to admit I am a little let down when we board the Delta hopper to Atlanta. It is about as big as a trailer and those first-class seats looked about like the other ones. I don't say a thing though and shut my mind up too. I've already decided I won't complain one bit and put a damper on Mama's gift to us, no matter what happens. Perk and Teddy fuss over who gets the window seat and I take my aisle seat across from them.

Once we're in the air I feel my excitement stirring.

With all the arrangements to be made in leaving for the trip I'd hardly had time to feel overwhelmed by the loss of Mama. Regular days had been filled up with Mama for so long I didn't have any idea what I would do now. With Mama dying, I thought I was losing a part of me I needed to survive. This trip came right when I needed it to, even if my nerves now are beginning to stir up faster than a bee buzzing by with the thought of being in the air.

The woman in the window seat beside me is sound asleep, as if flying is the most common thing in the world. Perk takes the glass of champagne the stewardess offers and Teddy orders a bourbon and coke. I am about to decline a drink when Perk says, "Have the champagne, Pauline, we have to toast Mama."

"It's not even noon, Perk," I tell her, "and we still have another flight to catch after this one."

"Oh, they don't leave first class behind," the woman beside me says.

Startled, I look over at her. I am not sure if she has just woken up or has been awake all along, resting her eyes.

"I'm Marion Conner." She smiles and looks directly at me, then over to Perk and adds, "the best time to drink champagne is in the air."

I smile nervously, sizing her up to be a little younger, in her fifties, with hair dyed blonde and a kind pair of brown eyes that twinkled like they held a secret. The last thing I want is to have small talk with a stranger, but something about this woman puts me at ease right away.

"I used to be an airline stewardess." She turns to look at me and winks. "For a minute." Marion starts laughing then and before long Perk is leaning over Teddy and laughing right along with her. Perk can talk to anyone. "I was collecting unemployment from my property management job that went under and I saw this ad in the paper, and I thought, well Marion you are fifty years old and no one is going to hire you as a stewardess. I was living in Norfolk then. I thought I would apply so I could get my quota of employment applications in for the week, you know, you had to apply for five jobs a week back then." Marion looks at each of us and nods.

Teddy and I take our glasses from the stewardess and Marion orders a vodka and orange juice and continues on.

"And do you know they hired me? Fifty years old. Remember Potomac Air, the BET network used to own them? Well they hired me and I went to training and I flew all up and down the East Coast." Marion is grinning about as wide as Perk, who sits across the aisle, laughing over her champagne.

"Until 9/11. I quit after that." Marion looks over at all of us and I can see the lines around her eyes. She might have looked younger at first glance, but the woman is easily Perk's age. I decide it's her pep that fools me.

Marion starts laughing again. "I drive a school bus now. My resume is about the size of a book, I've done so many things, but you know, this is the only life I get and while I'm here I am going to live it up. I'm headed down to Mexico to visit a friend, she started up a yoga studio in San Miguel. Can you imagine, yoga in the Mexico mountains?" Marion laughs again, shaking her head. "Why not, I say, go teach yoga in Mexico if that floats your boat?"

"Why not?" I add, and before I can even look over at Perk, I am laughing, feeling a lightness that only comes with freedom, freedom from worry and fret, freedom to laugh with my whole heart. I feel it and I know it's time, time to let that freedom in. Time to forgive myself. All the emptiness filling me with Mama gone seems in the distance now, as if she is right here inside me, enjoying herself, filling me back up with her love, encouraging me to live my life, live it up.

Marion is still laughing but stops when she looks down at her feet, brushes something off of her shoes, and then bends down to look at my shoes, Mama's old loafers, that I've decided to bring along with me.

"Oh my goodness, you have on loafers just like my mother wore up until she died. I tried more than once to take them for myself and every time she told me no, you are going to bury me first." Marion laughs and adds, "and I did just that, buried her and brought those old shoes back to my house. They are about as comfortable as a shoe can be and you know what, I feel like she is right there with me when I wear them. I'm not going to lie, I talk to her sometimes."

I look at Marion and my eyes get wide and a droplet runs down my cheek and in a voice about as low as a whisper, I say, "I know." We both smile then and nod. There are some things you can't explain, but if you believe them, they are true.

The stewardess walks back and hands Marion her drink, and the four of us toast. To Mama. To living it up. By the time we've landed in Atlanta and Marion has gone off in one direction and we've gone off in another, Marion and I have exchanged phone numbers and addresses and made plans for the four of us to meet for dinner, once we're all back in Richmond.

For once, I am making the plans.

As we hurry to meet our next connection, my pace slows a little, and I catch myself smiling even as tears stream down my face. "Living it up, Mama style," I say to Mama, to Perk and Teddy, to me.

Epilogue

MAMA IS STILL IN THE JELLY CABINET in Perk's basement, poured loosely into the cloisonne jar she bought on her honeymoon in San Francisco. Antiques both of them, the jelly cabinet was her grandmother's, my great-grandmother Zora Bell, who put up every berry jelly and jam she could find in the hills and mountains around Roanoke. Perk irons and does laundry in her basement and talks to Mama daily. The jelly cabinet, worn walnut panels and spindly legs, sits patiently, always upright, and Mama rests inside.

It's been a year since Mama died, and the cousins have called and asked more than a few times when the memorial will be. Perk and I agree, we'll have it before Mama turns 100. She was 97 when she died. We've got a little more time. I couldn't tell you though if that cloisonné jar will ever give up all of Mama's ashes. Perk has come to depend on her, talking to her, feeling her presence through the jelly cabinet in the cloisonné jar.

I talk to Mama too, feel her often, even though her solid remains rest at Grove Avenue. Just yesterday, I found a pair of her polyester pants hanging in the back of my closet and, as I folded them, and stacked them on the dresser, ready to be placed in the donation bin, I touched them and said, "Hi,

Mama." They are still there, and I still say "Hi" whenever I'm strolling by, and give them a little pat. Mama's loafers are still in the hallway, and even though they haven't moved, they still glow. I slip them on anytime I feel a pang of loneliness.

There is Mama in all the corners of my sister and me.

Acknowledgments

THANK YOU TO MY EARLY READERS, Betsy Fletcher, Susan Caudill, Molly O-Dell, Ann and Jim Wilson, Lisa McKnight, and Patricia Kinser, for your insights and encouragement.

Lisa and Patricia, thank you for your patience and persistence through multiple drafts and your great insights.

A huge thanks to my editor, Elizabeth Ferris, for showing me the path to the story and patiently waiting for me to find it.

Anna Benn, my editor at Torchflame Books, thank you for encouraging me to dive deeper and for finding all the holes.

To all the folks at Torchflame Books, thank you for giving this novel a home. I am forever grateful.

About the Author

LEE SOWDER GREW UP in Roanoke, Virginia, and now lives in Richmond, Virginia. She graduated college with a BS in Sociology from James Madison University and received a post-baccalaureate certificate in Information Technology from Virginia Commonwealth University.

Lee's careers have included Youth Counselor, Realtor, Claims Processor, and several Information Technology positions.

Now retired, Lee enjoys writing and has developed her writing skills in the Life in Ten Minutes writing workshops. Her poetry and prose have been published in the *Life in Ten Minutes Literary Magazine*.

Family Weave is Lee's debut. Look for her next novel, coming soon.

Connect with Lee:

Twitter @SowderLee
Facebook:/leesowder
Instagram @leesowder

CPSIA information can be obtained
at www.ICGtesting.com
Printed in the USA
BVHW031924180121
598071BV00010B/437